THE POWER OF

Passion

DENNIS W.C. WONG

ISBN: 978-1-954341-26-5 (Paperback)

The views expressed in this book are solely those of the author and do not necessarily reflect the views of the publisher, and the publisher hereby disclaims any responsibility for them.

BRANDING

Writers' Branding
1800-608-6550
www.writersbranding.com
orders@writersbranding.com

*Dedicated to Rae Chukwu,
my Nigerian soul sister.*

"My Journey"

My journey is just beginning,
Continuing,
With no ending.

Searching for a meaning,
Reasoning,
With an understanding.

I reach out to you assisting,
Comforting,
With care providing.

Embracing each day smiling,
Never ending,
With a new beginning.

Dennis W.C. Wong
April 24, 2002

CONTENTS

Chapter One   Could this be love 1
Chapter Two   Kate can you stop, please 25
Chapter Three This is outrageous 47
Chapter Four   Good morning, sweetie 71
Chapter Five   This is tough... 91

INTRODUCTION

Passion fruit is the fruit of Passiflora edulis vine. The two main characters, Passiflora a.k.a. Flora and Edulis a.k.a. Eddie, started out their relationship as a casual encounter that leads to their passionate love for each other. The story picks up when they are engaged couple. Everyone can have a passion for success in life and love. I am hoping that the fruits of my labor may someday benefit my children and their children.

CHAPTER ONE

Could this be love, and obsession, collage, or both? Could it have withstood myriads of albatrosses too? Was it to be an obsession that wouldn't fade away at the instance of the slightest hindrance?

It was a bright day in April as the clocks struck 4 p.m., edging towards evening. Eddie had just returned to his house in time to prepare himself in anticipation of his fiancée's scheduled visit. Flora, his fiancée, was expected to visit him that day as he wanted to use the opportunity to introduce her to his mother. However, he hadn't informed his mother of the impending visit. As a result, his mother, Mrs. Kate, who came for a visit, was surprised to see her son at home by that time. It was an unusual time for him to be home during work hours.

Usually, his work schedule was between the hours of 8 a.m. and 6 p.m., but on this fateful day, it was different – the love of his life was about to visit, and she rarely did. On the occasions she had been there, she had neither ventured into his bedroom nor stayed beyond thirty minutes. This day though, she had promised Eddie she would be spending quality time with him and his mother.

"Good afternoon, Mom," Eddie greeted when he saw his mother seated in the sitting room, busy with the Chinese program showing on the television. She was a woman who watched only either Chinese program or Chinese-related programs. To her, other than being Chinese, every other television content was a waste of time.

"Good afternoon, Ed," Mrs. Kate responded while fiddling with the remote control of the television to bring down the volume. "Ed" was her pet name for her son, Eddie.

"Why are you home so early? Hope there is no problem. Or are you ill?" Mrs. Kate added after she had brought down the TV volume. She was perturbed as she rose from the sofa, placing her right hand on Eddie's forehead to feel his temperature.

"Mom, I am fine," Eddie replied, smiling.

"So, why are you home at this time of the day?" Mrs. Kate asked.

"Mom, someone special is coming here today. I just can't wait for you to see her. I am sorry I didn't inform you earlier," Eddie said, smiling.

"And who could that be?" Mrs. Kate asked.

"The woman I want to marry, Flora is her name. You know, I once mentioned her to you. Have you forgotten so soon, Mom?" Eddie asked.

"Oh, I remember. That's nice. In that case, I need to get things ready. I can't wait to see my son's fiancée," Mrs. Kate said, smiling as she walked straight to the kitchen while Eddie walked into his room to remove his clothes and wear his casual outfit. He made it to the kitchen to join his mother as he was very fond of her.

"Your dad called," Mrs. Kate said, though listlessly, as she kept on stirring the soup.

"Oh, nice. I wish Dad was here to see Flora," Eddie said, grinning.

"I will be going back home by the weekend," Mrs. Kate said.

"Are you missing him?" Eddie asked, looking into his mother's eyes.

"I am not. I just need to go home, that's all," Mrs. Kate replied, betraying a little frown on her face.

"You know, I have always wanted to ask you why you always get upset every time I ask whether you love or miss Dad. Is there anything I should know that you're not telling me?" Eddie asked, stealing a glance at his mother.

"Let me go and set the table while you go to your room to have your bath," Mrs. Kate said, trying to change the subject as she walked out of the kitchen. Eddie followed suit as he made straight for his bedroom where he quickly went into the bathroom to freshen up. Soon after, he was finished, coming out of the bathroom to dry his body and put on a pair of black jeans and a blue t-shirt. He was still combing his hair when he got a call, and on checking the caller, he found out it was Flora. He picked it up immediately.

"Hi, darling," Eddie exclaimed as he picked up his call.

"Hi, love. I'm at the door," Flora announced.

Eddie closed the phone promptly and left his room towards the entrance door. Flora was standing there looking stunning, beautiful, and gorgeous as ever.

"Wow! You look beautiful, my love," Eddie complimented, half hugging her while holding the door wide open for her to come inside. They both walked to the sitting room to meet Mrs. Kate, who embraced Flora. Immediately she sighted her, pursing her mouth into a prim expression, obviously excited and happy at her son's choice of a wife.

"You look wonderful," Mrs. Kate said, grinning and meaning every word of it.

"Thanks, Mom," Flora replied shyly.

"You're welcome, my daughter. Shall we go into the dining room? "

"Oh, sure," Flora acquiesced as they all walked to the dining table.

Mrs. Kate took time to dish out the food and upon tasting the soup, Flora was quick to heap praises on Mrs. Kate for indeed the traditional Chinese soup she made tasted nice. She was a great cook.

"Ed has told me so much about you, and I have always wanted to see you, Flora. So, tell me which part of China are you from?" Mrs. Kate asked, eyeing Flora.

If only Flora knew that her response would set a chain reaction of events in her relationship with her soon to be mother-in-law. If only she knew how out of touch with modern times the woman sitting next to her was. If only she knew, she would have made herself Chinese.

"I am not from China. I'm from Hawaii," Flora replied with a tinge of pride.

The reaction from Mrs. Kate was instantaneous. It was without any form of pretense whatsoever. Her once glowing, smiling face became a visage of a contorted frown. She dropped her spoon on the table instantly while casting a bitter, sad glance at her son seated opposite her.

"Is there any problem, Mom?" Eddie asked, bewildered, as he was quick to notice the sudden change of countenance.

"I thought she was Chinese," Mrs. Kate said as she rose from the table.

"No, she is not. You heard it from her," Eddie replied as Mrs. Kate shifted the dining chair back and stood up.

"Where are you going?" Eddie asked, mouth agape.

"To my room, of course!" The tone of response from Mrs. Kate was a bit higher than usual, showing she was agitated.

"But you barely touched your soup," Eddie observed.

"I have no appetite to eat anymore," Mrs. Kate said and walked out of the table.

"Obviously, everything is not okay. This is not good," Flora muttered to herself, audible enough for Eddie to hear.

"Yeah, but don't worry. Let's finish up," Eddie assured her, as he continued with his soup but lost in thoughts.

Flora became uncomfortable with what happened but she slowly continued eating her food. Eddie requested she wait in the sitting room while he cleared the table. Flora rose from her seat, ready to leave.

"Why are you leaving so early?" Eddie asked.

"It seems your mother doesn't like me. I mean, I am not blind. I saw the facial expression on her face when she found out I wasn't Chinese. Her face spoke a million languages, and I understood it very clearly. Of course, there is nothing I can do about it. Should I have lied to her and said that I was Chinese? Our nationalities are one of the many things in life we have no control over. Perhaps you need to make her understand that while I take my leave," Flora replied.

"I also observed that, and it came after showing her likeness for you. She hugged you when you came in and said some nice things to you, and then the sudden change on hearing you are Hawaiian..."

"Yea, her likeness for me and her niceties faded like a bubble as soon as she heard the word Hawaii. There wouldn't have been any nice words nor any likeness in the first place," Flora replied, cutting Eddie short.

"Well, let me still pretend that's the problem until I hear from her. I will talk to her myself, but whatever may be the case, it's you that I love, and it's you that I will marry. That's my final decision, and no one can change that, not even my mother," Eddie said defiantly.

"Alright, my love, but still then I need to leave while you talk to your mom. Take care of yourself, my dear," Flora said as she walked out of the house. Eddie sighed and walked to his mother's room to talk with her.

"Mom, what's the problem? Why did you leave like that? Why the sudden change? Why the embarrassment to my fiancée?" Eddie asked as soon as he sat down on the chair in the visitor's room, where his mother stayed.

"Has she left?" Those were the words that left Mrs. Kate's lips, almost in whispers. She was disturbed.

"Yes, Mom. So, what's the problem?" Eddie asked.

"You can't marry her, Ed. No, you can't," Mrs. Kate said.

"Why? Why can't I marry the woman of my choice?" Eddie asked.

"Simple. Flora isn't one of us. Can't you see? She isn't Chinese. She doesn't deserve you. There are lots of pretty Chinese girls out there you can get married to, and I can even get one for you." Mrs. Kate said.

"What's wrong with Flora, Mom?" Eddie asked.

"Nothing other than the fact that she is isn't Chinese, that's what's wrong with her," Mrs. Kate answered.

"This is hilarious! I mean, in this 21st century? So, you mean I should dump my soulmate simply because she isn't the same nationality as me? How cruel of you? Well, she is the one I love and nothing can change that. The sooner you accept her, the better for all of us because she is the only one that I love and would want to spend the rest of my life with," Eddie said.

"You can't marry her, and that's final. You're my son, and you have to obey me," Mrs. Kate insisted.

"Yes, there is no denying the fact that I'm your son. That's a fact, and I have always obeyed you, but on this issue, you're not the one to make my choice for me on the choice of a life partner. I'll be the one making that choice. She is everything I want in a woman. She is my other half and I don't think I can love another the way I love her," Eddie said.

"Hawaiians are evil. She is evil," Mrs. Kate intoned.

"What! Really! What did you just say now? Why this stereotyping of every Hawaiian as evil? Well, for your information, in case you haven't known it, Flora is the sweetest thing ever if you get to know her, and there are lots of Hawaiians like her. Hawaiians are not evil!" Eddie fired back, still managing to smile, though.

"That's the problem. Flora has bewitched you already, just as I suspected. But I can't fold my hands to see that happen. I don't want to know if you feel she is an angel. I simply don't want her to be around you. She doesn't deserve you, and that's final," Mrs. Kate maintained.

"I can't believe these words are coming from you, Mom. It's just incredible. Flora loves me, and I love her, too. What else matters?" Eddie said, softening down a bit.

Mrs. Kate got up from where she sat on the bed and walked closer to Eddie, tenderly holding his hand as she spoke in a low, loving tone: "Ed, can't you just see? She is not the one for you. If she were, she would have been Chinese. You can't marry her. You're my son and I know what's good for you. Flora isn't good for you."

Eddie looked at his Mom and gently extricated his hand from her grip, rising to his feet and looking at his Mom directly in her eyes, said, "It's Flora who I am spending my forever with. If you can't accept that, then that's really your headache, not mine." Hardly had he finished speaking, then he stormed out of the room.

Mrs. Kate sat back on the bed, feeling dejected.

"He can't get married to her. Why can't he listen to me, so everything ends here?" Mrs. Kate whined, angrily muttering to herself.

As soon as Eddie left his mom, he walked straight to his room, where he sat dejectedly on his bed and dialed Flora's number, but she didn't pick up. He dropped the phone and settled down on the bed, lying face up.

"What's wrong with Mom? Why is she treating Flora this way?" Eddie soliloquized as his mind roved over the possible reasons for his mom's bias. He kept glancing at the ceiling before he drifted off to sleep.

****

"Ed, wake up." Mrs. Kate said while tapping his son. Eddie opened his eyes slowly and he saw his mother standing over him. "Is there any problem?" He demanded, sitting up.

"I want to talk to you, and besides, it's already 6 p.m. You need to wake up so you can sleep later at night," Mrs. Kate said. Eddie stood up and walked into the bathroom to wash his face, coming out a few minutes later to sit at the edge of the bed, attentive to whatever his mom had to say.

"You wanted to talk to me, Mom. I am all ears," He began.

"It's about Flora," Mrs. Kate said.

"Ooh! Not again!" Eddie said, frowning, shifting uneasily on the edge of the bed.

"Listen, my son, I will never mislead you nor will I ever make the wrong decision for you. You're my son, and your happiness matters a lot to me. You see, Flora isn't the right woman for you. Hawaiians are no good. They can make your life miserable. I can go out there and get a pretty Chinese woman for you who is ten times better than Flora," Mrs. Kate concluded as she waited on Eddie to respond. For what seemed like an hour, Eddie has still yet to speak. Mrs. Kate was becoming edgy when she heard Eddie's voice, slow but steady, quite unlike her son's voice.

"I am not disputing the fact that there are other women out there who look better than Flora but I don't want them, and I will never go for them. Seriously, I don't understand why you won't let this matter be. The reason you're giving is a non-issue as far as I'm concerned. It's Flora or no one else. If this was the reason you woke me, I am sorry, but it won't work, Mom," Eddie said as he picked up his phone and made for the door.

"Where are you going?" Mrs. Kate asked.

"I want to have some breath of fresh air, Mom." He replied and walked out of the room. He went to the balcony, sat on the cushion there, brought out his phone from his pocket, and discovered he missed Flora's call. He quickly called back and she picked it immediately on the first ring.

"Darling, I'm sorry I missed your call. You called when I was sleeping," Eddie apologized.

"That's not a problem. I thought so, that's why I didn't bother to call again. I know you always pick up my calls on the first ring once you're with your phone," Flora said.

"How are you doing?" Eddie asked.

"I am great. When you called earlier, I wasn't with my phone. I was trying to prepare food," Flora explained.

"That's alright. I just wanted to find out whether you safely got back home," Eddie said.

"Okay, thanks, my dear. So, did you get to find out the reason for your mother's sudden change in attitude, other than the fact that I am Hawaiian and not Chinese? If I have to apologize for anything, I'm ready to do so," Flora said.

"You did no wrong. But, darling, why didn't you ask God to make you Chinese so that my mom can approve of you? Hahaha! My mom is not serious. I don't know why that should be an issue, but that's her business and not mine. What matters is that I love you and that it's you I'm going to marry," Eddie said.

"But she is your mother!" Flora countered.

"I know, but that doesn't mean she will decide who I will end up with for the rest of my life. It's you or no one else, and you don't have to worry yourself about this. Sooner or later, she will have no choice but to accept and respect my choice," Eddie said.

"Alright, dear. I just hope things end up well for us," Flora said.

"Sure. Please don't get bothered about this, alright?" Eddie begged.

"Okay, I will try not to. Take care of yourself," Flora said.

"And you too," Eddie said and cut the phone off. After spending close to two hours on the balcony, Eddie went inside to have his dinner. His food was already on the dining table waiting for him. He sat down and ate quietly. When he finished, he took the dishes inside the kitchen and washed them before placing them on the plate rack. He walked back into his room, took out his pajamas, and laid them on the bed. Then he hurriedly had his bath, wore his pajamas, and said his prayers before drifting off to sleep.

****

Mrs. Kate turned her back to see who tapped her and discovered it was Flora. Both of them were in the market to get some food items some weeks after their encounter at Eddie's house.

"Good afternoon, ma'am. How are you doing?" Flora curtseyed, smiling.

Mrs. Kate kept mute while casting a furtive glance at her. Flora interpreted this action as meaning non-recognition of her by Mrs. Kate as she went on to explain who she was.

"It's me, Flora, your son's fiancée," Flora explained.

"I know who you are, Flora," Mrs. Kate abruptly cut her short.

"I'm not that deft not to have recognized the one who wants to take my son's heart away, the Hawaiian! Oh yes, I know you. And about getting married to my son, Ed, forget it. I already got someone else for him, and they are both at home now," Mrs. Kate said.

"That's not possible. Eddie said he loves me and he would marry me," Flora countered, almost at the point of breaking down.

"I hope you also know that I am Ed's mother and that he listens to anything I say. You're not part of us, and you can never be, so stop trying to fit in. You're not Chinese, Flora. My son can never marry you, and the earlier you realized that, the better for you," Mrs. Kate said and walked out on Flora, leaving her transfixed on the spot, speechless but in tears.

She quickly dried the tears trickling down her cheeks as she continued with what she came to buy, though mostly absentmindedly.

****

"Mom, you came back so early?" Eddie observed as Mrs. Kate came into the house.

She quietly sat down, took a quick look at her son and nodded her head countless times, suggestively, while dropping her bag on the tiled floor.

"Why are you looking at me and nodding your head like that? What's the problem? Did anything go wrong? Say something, please," Eddie pleaded.

"Hmm, you can't believe who I saw today," Mrs. Kate began.

"Who was that?" Eddie asked, eyeing her.

"I saw Flora with a guy who claimed to be her fiancé, and when I tried to confirm it from her, she pretended as if she doesn't know me and simply walked away with the man," Mrs. Kate said.

"That's hilarious. You're not serious, right? You might have seen someone else," Eddie said, laughing out loud.

"Do you think I will come back home to fabricate lies to you? Your so-called Flora is going to marry someone else," Mrs. Kate almost shouted.

Eddie looked at his mother before picking up his phone to call Flora's number, but she didn't pick up at first which prompted him to call again, and then she picked up.

"Darling!" Eddie called out.

"Don't you ever call my number again, you liar," Flora shouted and turned the phone off.

Eddie was taken aback at her words. He wondered what could have caused that. He tried calling her number countless times but she didn't pick up.

"I told you she isn't the right person for you and that there was something odd about your Flora. She isn't the one. There are many Chinese girls out there that I can get for you to marry, but you refused to heed to my voice," Mrs. Kate said.

"You said you saw her with a man. I called her, but she called me a liar, without even hearing any word from me. I don't understand what's going on, but obviously, something is amiss, something is wrong somewhere, and I need to fix it," Eddie said while still clutching his phone.

"There is nothing wrong. You have to accept the truth that Flora doesn't love you one bit, just like all Hawaiians, a deceptive lot they are. She is only trying to pass the time with you. Don't kill yourself over that. I will get someone better for you," Mrs. Kate said.

"I don't need anyone else, Mom. It's Flora I want, but I need to find out what the problem is," Eddie said as he walked back into his room, still dialing Flora's number but she remained adamant about not picking up his call.

"Oh my God, what's happening?" Eddie was now very much worried, sighing as he sat on his bed while still dialing Flora's number once again. She turned her phone off. Out of despair, he flung his phone on the bed, shouting: "This can't be happening." His phone's ringing tone distracted him as he checked to find out who the caller was and found out it was his colleague at his workplace.

"Ethan, how are you doing?" Eddie asked as soon as he picked up the phone.

"Man, I'm cool, but your voice sounds like someone agitated. Is everything okay?" Ethan asked.

"Nothing much. I am fine, man," Eddie assured.

"Alright, if you say so. I sent something to your mail. Do go through it and get back to me," Ethan said.

"Alright, I will do that now," Eddie said.

"Are you sure you don't want to talk about what's bothering you?" Ethan asked.

"It's Flora," Eddie conceded.

"What about her?" Ethan asked.

"Mom said she saw her with another man who claimed to be her fiancé and that Flora pretended as if she doesn't know her. Then I tried calling her but she called me a liar when she picked up my call even without hearing anything from me. She asked me not to call her again and hung up the phone. I've tried calling her back, but she turned the phone off," Eddie explained, clearly worried.

"Do you think she is having an affair with someone else?" Eddie added.

"I don't think so, Eddie. She is one of the best things that has ever happened to you, and on counting your blessings, you need to count her twice. I suggest you go over to her place and know what the problem is. You don't have to sit there in your house and conclude. I mean, the man who claimed to be her fiancé could be a relative, simply pulling a trick," Ethan advised.

"Alright, I will do that tomorrow as it is already dark. I just don't want to lose Flora for anything in this world," Eddie said.

"Did you offend her in any way?" Ethan asked.

"No, I can't remember hurting her," Eddie said.

"Then why would she call you a liar?" Ethan asked.

"That's the problem, and I seriously don't know Ethan. I just feel something is wrong somewhere," Eddie said.

"That's the more reason you have to go over to her place and sort it out," Ethan chided.

"Thank you so much, man," Eddie said.

"You're welcome," Ethan replied.

"I will go through the mail and get back to you," Eddie said and hung up.

He tried calling Flora's number once again. He sighed and kept the phone on the bed as he stood up, walked out of the room, and went straight to the kitchen. He opened the refrigerator, took out a bottle of water to drink, and then turned to his mom who was sitting on a chair and slicing onions.

"Flora's line is off. I can't reach her anymore," Eddie said to his mom.

"She has moved on, you too should do the same," Mrs. Kate said.

"She hasn't moved on. I just think there is a mix up somewhere and I will fix it by tomorrow," Eddie curtly said.

"Interesting. Then why did Flora switch off her phone?" Mrs. Kate asked.

"It's obvious she is angry about something she feels I'm guilty of, the reason she wouldn't want to talk to me. You said you saw her with a man. How sure are you the man isn't her brother or relative?" Eddie asked.

"By the time you realized the truth, it will be late for you, and that's when she will be here to drop off her wedding invitation card for you," Mrs. Kate said, smiling.

"You're just not helping matters," Eddie said and walked out of the kitchen. He went back to his room, dialed Flora's younger brother's line and it went through.

"Hello, Jason! Is Flora there?" Eddie asked immediately.

"Yeah, she is in her room. She came back home from the market feeling moody, looking upset. She then ran into her room and since then, she hasn't stepped out. She won't tell anyone what the problem is," Jason replied.

"I have been calling her number and it isn't going through," Eddie said.

"I think she switched it off," Jason replied.

"I want to ask you something of which I need you to tell me the truth, and mind you, this stays between us," Eddie said.

"Alright, man, go on," Jason said.

"Is Flora having an affair with someone else?"

"No, she isn't. She doesn't double date. Why would you even believe that? You're the only man she has brought home," Jason answered, sounding a bit upset at Eddie's question.

"I need you to keep her at home tomorrow, I will be coming by 7 a.m.," Eddie said.

"Alright, I will," Jason said.

"Thank you," Eddie said and ended the call.

****

Eddie had woken up to the noise from his ringing tone and upon checking, he discovered it was Jason. He picked up immediately.

"Good morning to you, Eddie." Jason greeted,

"Good morning," Eddie replied, yawning.

"Can you please come over here right away? Flora wants to travel and stay with a distant relative. I don't know when she will be back. I'm trying to talk to her to slow her down before you get here," Jason said.

"Oh, thanks, man. I'm coming over there right now. Please just hold Flora back for me. I'll be there before you know it," Eddie said and hung up.

He checked the time and discovered it was already 6 a.m. and quickly climbed down the bed as he rushed into the bathroom to have his bath. He wore his jean trousers with a red t-shirt on top, grabbing his car keys as he raced out of the house. He was still trying to unlock the car when he discovered he left his house's front door open. He went back to lock it close before leaving.

He got to Flora's place in less than forty minutes and found a suitable spot to park as he alighted from his vehicle, locking it. Jason walked up to him immediately as soon as he sighted him.

"Don't tell me that I am late," Eddie said.

"Somehow, Flora is already down with her suitcase. She is yours to talk to, anyway," Jason said as the duo rushed inside the house together. When the door opened, Flora thought it was her younger brother, asking him to come and help her with her luggage.

"You're traveling somewhere?" Eddie said. Flora remained frozen to the spot but eventually turning to face Eddie.

"Why are you here? Who let you in here?" She shouted.

"Can we at least sit down and talk?" Eddie pleaded.

"Sit and talk about what exactly? That one minute you claimed to love me and the next minute, you are with another woman simply because I'm not Chinese? Do you think I wasn't going to find out?" She fired at Eddie, with every bitterness in her. "What are you talking about?" Eddie asked.

"Oh please, don't try to feign ignorance and act like you don't know what I'm saying. You have moved on because your Mom didn't accept me. What else exactly are you doing here because I don't understand what you want to talk about..." Flora was saying when Jason, who came in through the door, interrupted her.

"Sister, can you please listen to what he has to say first."

"Jason, please allow her to speak. Otherwise, I won't know what my crime is," Eddie said as he remained standing facing Flora.

"You're a cheat, and I need you to leave my house this instant," Flora said in her intense outburst.

"I will leave on one condition, Flora. First, you have to tell me who told you I was having an affair with someone else or what makes you think so," Eddie said.

"Fine. You want the truth? I met your mother in the market and she told me you're with the woman you want to marry in the house and that I shouldn't bother trying to fit in because I will never belong to you or your family, that she has already got a Chinese lady for you," Flora said as tears trickled down her cheeks.

"What! You mean, my mom told you that?" Eddie asked.

"What? Are you surprised or you think the truth will remain hidden forever?" Flora continued.

"What silly truth are you talking about, Flora? She lied to you and you fell for it. You couldn't even call me to confirm what she said," Eddie shouted at her for the first time since they had been together.

"What are you saying?" Flora quietly asked, softening down, completely ashamed of herself, of her naivety.

"What she told you was the same thing she told me. She lied to me that she met you in the market with another man who claimed to be your fiancé," Eddie said.

"Was that the reason you asked me if Flora was having an affair with someone else?" Jason asked.

"Yes, that's the reason, and beyond this, Flora, we have known each other for some years now. When she told you that, you should have called or better still, come to the house to see the woman in question for yourself," Eddie said.

"What's that? Where to?" Flora mopped at him, surprised.

"I am sorry, darling. Please forgive me. I was beclouded by rage, by disbelief. I was confused," Flora apologized as Eddie walked closer to her and cleaned the tears drizzling down her cheek, hugging her in the process, a hug of assurance, but suddenly disengaging from the hug and walking away.

"I have an issue to settle with Mom," Eddie said and left the house as he rushed into his car and sped off.

Immediately he got home, he rushed into the kitchen and met his mother cooking.

"What were you trying to gain from all these, mom?" Eddie shrilled at his mother.

"What are you saying?" Mrs. Kate asked.

"Don't act like you don't know what I am saying. Why would you lie to Flora and still get back to lie to me? What if you had succeeded and Flora ended up leaving me?" Eddie asked.

"Then I would have been the happiest person alive," Mrs. Kate said.

"Can you hear yourself, Mom? Will you be the happiest person while your son wallows in pain and misery? Is this what you call love?" Eddie asked.

"Flora will never get married to you. I will end that marriage before it starts," Mrs. Kate threatened.

"And before you end it, you would have to go back home. Don't try to ruin the home I am trying to build with Flora. You already have yours, please allow me to have mine, Mom!" Eddie yelled the more.

"So, you want me to leave your house because of that girl, Flora? You aren't even married to her yet and she is already in full control of you. What other explanation do you need that this girl just isn't the right person for you?" Mrs. Kate asked.

"I don't need any explanation, Mom. The only explanation here is that you are out to end this relationship and I won't fold my hands and let it happen. This is my life, and you have to learn to respect my choice. If eventually, I felt I made a mistake or a bad choice, needing your advice, trust me, I will come to you. But for now, I don't need it and you have to respect that," Eddie said.

"You won't get married to her," Mrs. Kate said.

"I will call Dad now and let him know that you're coming home," Eddie said and walked out of the kitchen.

****

Mrs. Janet had called Eddie to pass across a message to Mrs. Kate, her twin sister, because she knew she was there in Eddie's house.

"Aunty, Good evening. How are you doing?" Eddie greeted his mom's twin sister, Mrs. Janet, over the phone.

"I am great, but you don't sound happy. What's the problem?" She asked.

"I am fine, Aunty," Eddie replied.

"I don't want to ask again," Mrs. Janet said, and Eddie did catch the tone of finality in her voice.

"It's Mom. She doesn't want me to marry my girl just because she isn't Chinese. Seriously, that's absurd and impossible because I am in love with her. I don't think I can love another woman," Eddie whined.

"Where is she from?" Mrs. Janet asked.

"Hawaii, and I've demanded from mom to know what's wrong with her being a Hawaiian," Eddie said.

"There is nothing wrong with that, Eddie. The most important thing is that you love and cherish her. As for my sister, I will talk to her," Mrs. Janet assured.

"That's not all. Mom saw Flora at the market and lied to her that I was with another woman at home, and once she got back home, she lied to me saying she saw Flora with another man. The first day Mom met Flora, she her with a huge dose of embarrassment simply because Flora is Hawaiian. Mom is ready to go to any length to make sure that she separates us, and that's not nice. Mom claims she loves me yet she doesn't care about my happiness. Flora is my happiness. I don't know why Mom is finding it hard to understand. I don't know what she will gain if Flora and I part ways. She just wants to ruin my life," Eddie complained.

"You mean she did all these?" Mrs. Janet asked with trembling lips.

"And she is threatening to do more just to achieve her aim of separating us. I'm just tired of her, so tired of her attitude. How could she be biased against a person, making sweeping statements against an entire people, lumping all of them together as being evil?" Eddie complained bitterly.

"Is she at home now?" Mrs. Janet asked.

"She already left. I asked her to since she is making herself a nuisance here. Besides, she has spent much time here with me, she needs to go look after Dad," Eddie said.

"Okay, then I'll have to meet with her at home and talk sense into her. Don't worry, son. She will eventually accept your girl," Mrs. Janet consoled.

"Thanks, Aunty. Even if she refused to heed your voice on this, I would still go ahead with the wedding plans. I am the one getting married to Flora, not her," Eddie insisted.

"Please don't be harsh on your mother. I am not saying what she is doing is right, but take things easy with her, okay?" Mrs. Janet pleaded.

"She is driving me crazy already," Eddie replied.

"Be calm. Everything will be right. I will come over, maybe during the weekend, so we can see and talk," Mrs. Janet said.

"I will appreciate that, Aunty. Do take care of yourself," Eddie said as he hung up and dialed Flora's number after. She picked up immediately.

"Hi, love!"

"How are you doing, darling?" Flora asked.

"I am fine, baby. I just got off the phone with my Aunty Janet. She promised to talk to my mom." Eddie said, evidently relieved.

"That's nice. I hope your mother agrees," Flora said.

"That's immaterial. Whether my mom agrees or not, it's none of her business. I am getting married to you and that's final. I am the one getting married to you and not her so she has no right to decide for me and to think that her only reason centers on nationality, not even something important. I mean, how can she demonize an entire nation?" Eddie said.

"Are you saying you will go ahead with the wedding plans, with or without her consent?" Flora asked.

"Hahaha! How many times will I say that or are you just pulling my leg? I know what I am doing, I know what I want. The person I want is you, no one else. I love you, we love each other, no one else's opinion matters," Eddie said.

"Hmmm, that's my prince charming, my armored knight. I am going to call you back in a few minutes," Flora said and was about to end the call when Eddie added, "Alright, no problem, just take care of yourself and henceforth stop listening to any negative talks from anyone, do you understand?"

"Yes, my dear. I will take care of myself, that's certain. Bye, my love," Flora said and ended the call.

Eddie stood up as he walked to the kitchen to prepare something to eat because he was famished. When he was done cooking and eating, he did the dishes. Later on, Eddie tried calling to check if his Mom had arrived safely home but his father picked it up. He was expecting his younger sister to answer the call.

"Ed, my son!" Matt, Eddie's father, exclaimed.

"Good evening, Dad. How are you doing?" Eddie asked.

"I am doing well," Matt replied.

"I called to find out if Mom arrived safely," Eddie said.

"Yes, she just got back a few minutes ago. Do you want to speak with her?" Matt asked.

"No, not now. I just wanted to find out if Mom got back home safely. I will call back later," Eddie said and hung up as he walked out of the house into the open air, happy with himself.

CHAPTER TWO

"Kate, can you stop, please! We are talking about your son. I understand that you love him, but you don't have to lie to the girl and him to have your way. That's not right at all. Where's your honor as a mother?" Mrs. Janet yelled at her twin sister. She visited her twin sister at home and tried talking to her about his son, but all fell on deaf ears as Mrs. Kate persisted in her unbridled hindrance to the union of her son with Flora.

"I don't want her," Mrs. Kate said

"But you're not the one getting married to her, Eddie is the one getting married to her. So, can't you see that your decision doesn't matter?" Mrs. Janet said.

"My opinion matters. Eddie is my son," Mrs. Kate swiftly countered.

"Oh yes, he is your son, but he is old enough to make decisions for himself. I hope you know that. Besides, why would you even lie to both of them? Why the manipulation? What were you thinking, Kate? What will you gain if you had succeeded in creating hostility between those two? Because I don't understand why they should do such, for crying out loud. Flora is a woman like you. Why are you trying to hurt her?" Mrs. Janet was saying. "Thank you, Aunty, for these questions. She is busy hurting someone else's daughter knowing full well she has a daughter like me at home," Anne, Eddie's younger sister who sat near Mrs. Janet, interjected.

"Will you keep quiet, Anne?" Mrs. Kate yelled.

"Allow her to air her views, Kate. Does the truth hurt you that bad? It's not nice, and it's coming from your daughter's mouth. Can't you see you're petty, Kate? You're hurting someone's daughter, knowing full well Anne will get married soon. It's not fair, just not fair. What happened to the sister I grew up with because you weren't like this when we were younger? Since you got married, you've been exuding so much pain and hatred. What's the problem? Is Flora the reason for your bitterness? Think of your son, think of his happiness," Mrs. Janet concluded.

"I don't want her, she isn't Chinese. She isn't part of us and she can't adapt," Mrs. Kate was adamant.

"How sure are you that Flora won't adapt? Is this not pettiness? I mean, she hasn't done anything wrong to you; the only thing you hold onto is your outdated idea of all Hawaiians being evil. You're just unreasonable, Kate," Mrs. Janet blurted out.

"Call it whatever you want. I don't care, but what I know is that Ed won't marry her, and that's final!" Mrs. Kate fumed.

"Mom, why are you so tribalistic? What's the problem with you? Why the hatred against an entire tribe, Mom?" Anne further chipped in.

"She isn't Chinese, that's the issue," Mrs. Kate replied.

"How sure are you that she does not have Chinese blood in her? Have you ever taken a closer look at her? If you did, you'd realize she looks like one of us," Anne said.

"She is Hawaiian, Anne. And all Hawaiians are evil," Mrs. Kate replied.

"She looks like Chinese and besides, does tribe matter in marriage? What's important is that they both love each other, and they are happy together. She is good for Eddie, and that's the most important thing," Anne replied.

"Can you just get out of here, Anne, since you don't have anything reasonable to contribute?" Mrs. Kate shouted.

"She is saying the truth, Kate. Even if you don't listen to me, at least listen to your daughter. Your son's happiness should matter a lot to you. He has already made his choice and it is yours to accept it," Mrs. Janet said with a frown creasing her brows.

"No one seems to understand me," Mrs. Kate said, gesticulating.

"Simple, because you're acting unreasonably in this matter. What's wrong with you, Kate? Is it because our parents chose our life partners for us? It doesn't mean you have the right to choose for your children also. Eddie is in love with Flora, and you need to accept that and move on," Mrs. Janet retorted. "Even if you all supported him and he still moves on with the wedding plans, just count me out of it because I won't be involved in it," Mrs. Kate furiously said and walked out on her twin sister.

"This is serious. Whatever the reason for this bias is getting grave. I don't know what it is, though. I just don't understand the reason for this bitterness," Anne said, wavering her head.

"She thinks because our parents did the same to us, she can do the same to Eddie without realizing that times have changed," Mrs. Janet fumed.

"Well, I know that in time she will realize the truth and just let things be," Anne calmly said.

"I should be going now, Anne. I am going to Eddie's place as I promised him that I would be coming to see him," Mrs. Janet said as she rose to go.

"That's nice, let me go with you then, and tomorrow I will come back home. Just a minute, let me pick my stuff," Anne said and dashed off to her room, coming back a few minutes later, clutching her handbag.

"Seems you're ready?" Mrs. Janet asked, smiling.

"Yes, I am," Anne said as both of them left the house.

****

Eddie was watching a TV series when the doorbell rang. He stood up from the sofa and walked toward the door to open it. Anne jumped and hugged Eddie tightly when the door flung open.

"You didn't tell me you were coming, Anne," Eddie observed, smiling.

"I just wanted to surprise you! And for your information, I'm not leaving today, it'll be tomorrow evening," Anne said, grinning, almost to the point of a grotesque grimace of a skull.

"Good evening, Aunty. Sorry, I was just surprised when I saw Anne with you," Eddie apologized.

"That's not an issue, Eddie. How are you doing?" Mrs. Janet asked.

"I'm doing great. No need to ask you both because I can see you both are looking great," Eddie said, smiling. He shut the door while Anne and Mrs. Janet sat on the sofa. Mrs. Janet was slumping down into it because she was an obese woman. Eddie walked into the kitchen and came back with a glass of juice, which he handed to his Aunty.

"Where is mine?" Anne asked.

"There's the kitchen, Anne. Help yourself to whatever you need," Eddie replied.

Anne sheepishly looked at him, not knowing what to say. She got up and walked into the kitchen.

"You know she is your little sister," Mrs. Janet jokingly chided Eddie.

"Yes, I do. Hahaha. It's her house too, so it's meant to feel free here. Go into any place without taking any permission from me." Eddie said, sitting down.

So, how are your children and your husband?" Eddie asked as he sat down next to Mrs. Janet.

"They are fine, Eddie. I left your family house a few hours ago, that's why Anne is here with me. She insisted on coming with me when I told her I was coming here," Mrs. Janet said.

"Oh, that's nice. Did Mom say anything?" Eddie fired the much anticipated question immediately.

"Nothing positive, but whatever it is, it has eaten deep into her system. I don't think she will accept Flora anytime soon, but that isn't the problem. You're happy with her and you love her. That's the most important thing," Mrs. Janet said.

"Thank you, Aunty," Eddie said, smiling broadly.

Anne walked out of the kitchen with a glass of juice. She sat down on the sofa opposite Eddie and Mrs. Janet and started sipping the drinks.

"Don't listen or pay attention to mom, whatever her problem is with Hawaiians is her business," Anne chipped in while relishing the excellent taste of the juice in her hands.

"Thanks, Anne," Eddie said, smiling.

"You're always welcome, brother," Anne responded, smiling.

"But I still feel I need to know something. Why is it that Mom gets pissed-off anytime I ask her about issues relating to Dad? She would always try to change the topic. Why?" Eddie pointedly asked Mrs. Janet.

"I thought I was the only one who observed that. But countless times I asked, and I never got a reply. Aunty Janet, do you know what the problem is? You're her twin sister, you may know," Anne asked.

"It started when we were still little, and it's not her fault. She was convinced into marrying someone she didn't like," Mrs. Janet said.

"Really? Tell me more about it," Eddie asked, drawing nearer to Mrs. Janet, really curious to hear the whole story.

"Our parents chose our husbands for us. When we were ripe for marriage, in my case, I eventually developed a love for my husband but Kate has since remained embittered by our father's action. Her heart is still with the love of her youth, the man she wanted to marry. So, that explains the reason for her aloofness over your father. She may have never loved him," Mrs. Janet concluded.

"Now I understand why all these things are happening. Your parents chose a husband for her and she thinks she can choose a wife for me. That's so not possible. Times have changed, and besides, I have grown to love and understand Flora. Leaving her for someone else is like starting life afresh. If she is sad in her marriage, then why does she wish the same for me?" Eddie asked.

"What happened? I want to hear everything," Anne asked.

"It's a long story, but I promise to make it short," Mrs. Janet said, smiling.

"Kate is the elder one between her and me. Our parents chose two suitors for my twin sister and me. She did not like your father, the man chosen for her. She wanted my man, but in Chinese culture, she can't be allowed to choose. We had no other option but to obey the custom and not question it. Kate and I were eventually married in Chinese Buddhist style when we were just fifteen years. The rest of our siblings chose whoever they wanted, but it wasn't for both of us. That's why she isn't always happy with your father. But the fact remains that they are married and nothing could have been done about it," Mrs. Janet added.

"Thank God I wasn't born in that era. Otherwise, I could have been married to someone else other than the one I love," Anne said, looking askance at the thought.

"I am happy for you and Stanley. At least mom won't have any issues with him, he is Chinese," Eddie said, smiling.

"Now I understand, but she should know that times are changing, and everyone is entitled to his or her own opinion," Eddie noted further.

"I don't think she will ever understand that," Anne said.

"She thinks we still live in that era but now she should allow you all to make your decision without trying to manipulate it. I know my sister. Though she is going to be a hard nut to crack, I know she will change sooner or later," Mrs. Janet assured.

"I hope so. I hope so," Eddie said, nodding his head repeatedly.

"It's getting late already. I need to start going now so I can get home on time," Mrs. Janet said, standing up.

"Anne, get up. We need to drop Aunty off," Eddie said as he grabbed his car keys. The trio walked outside. They all entered the vehicle and Eddie drove off. He dropped his aunt at the exact spot to get a cab back home and they waited till the driver drove off before driving back home. On their home, Eddie thought of veering off the road to see Flora. He had missed her since they saw each other last, and she was feeling lonely for having not seen Eddie for some days now.

"Why don't we stop at Flora's place to say hello to her," Anne suggested as if she read Eddie's mind.

"Hmmm, that's nice. Let me call Flora first to make sure she is at home," said Eddie as he fumbled for his phone tucked away in his hip pocket while looking for a cool spot to park his car. As soon he parked, he picked up his phone and dialed Flora's line who picked it on the first ring. She told him to come over right away and that she was at home. Eddie told her he was coming over with her younger sister, Anne.

"So, we are going over there, right?" Anne asked immediately. Eddie ended the call.

"Oh, yes, we are," Eddie said with evident excitement as he reignited the engine and drove down the street to Flora's house. A few minutes after they got to their destination, they descended and walked inside. In the sitting room, Jason greeted them and asked them to wait while he informed Flora of their arrival. Flora was inside doing some cleaning when Jason came to tell her of Eddie's presence. Upon hearing the news, her face lightened up and she dropped whatever she was doing to follow Jason into the sitting room.

"Good evening, my love," Flora greeted as she walked into the sitting room.

Eddie stood up to hug her upon seeing her, as Anne also stood up to hug her too.

"Anne, how are you doing?" Flora asked, turning to Anne as they hugged each other.

"I'm okay, Flora. Nice to see you once again," Anne said, grinning.

"We just dropped our Aunty off so we decided to drop by," Eddie offered as he held Flora by the hand to sit her down beside himself.

"Wow! That's thoughtful of you, darling. Did she succeed in talking to your mother?" Flora whispered to Eddie.

"You don't have to whisper, Anne knows everything, and everyone is talking to Mom, including Anne. As for Aunty, she tried talking to Mom too, but she wouldn't budge. She's just fixated on what she said earlier, but that's not a problem," Eddie said, assuring Flora as he drew her closer to himself.

"Wow! I thought she would accept me after Aunty Janet must have talked to her," Flora said, feeling sad.

"She isn't the one marrying you, I am. We heard from Aunty Janet how both of them were match mated by their parents to marry someone they didn't love, and it's obvious to Mom that she still thinks we are at the same age where she has the right to choose a life partner for us. Just because a husband was chosen for her doesn't mean she will do the same to me also. Times are changing," Eddie said.

"Thank you for standing up for me, my armored knight," Flora said, smiling and at the same time dropping tears of joy.

"Don't worry. I know my brother is going to get married to you, okay?" Anne assured, smiling.

"Thank you so much, Anne. You're a dear one," Flora said, heaving a sigh of relief.

"You're welcome, Flora," Anne replied as she immediately shifted to what she was watching on the TV, allowing Eddie to chit-chat with Flora as they spoke in whispers, laughing and smiling in between. Shortly after, Flora got up from the sofa and strolled into the kitchen to come out with some delicious rice on beautiful bowls, handing each bowl over to Eddie and Anne. They sat there in the sitting room to eat while Anne was eating and watching the TV. Eddie and Flora were still engaged in their chit-chat as they ate. Eddie and Flora went outside to have some private talk after eating, leaving Anne alone in the sitting room. As soon as they came back into the house, Eddie tapped Anne, who was still much engrossed in the movie showing on the TV.

"It's time to go," he said. They bid goodbyes to themselves. Eddie and Anne got into the car outside and zoomed off. When they got home, Anne didn't bother preparing anything as his brother had already had enough food in Flora's house. She went into the guest room, had her bath, and wore her nightwear. While lying down on the bed, she took out her phone, switched it on, and called Stanley, her fiancé.

"Anne, my darling, where have you been? I've been trying to call your number for God knows how many times now, but it's turned off. I even wanted to come to the house," Stanley said as soon as he answered her call.

"I'm so sorry, my love. I didn't know my phone had been off. Just saw it now that I brought it out from my handbag. I'm at Eddie's place now. I'll be home tomorrow. It was just an impromptu visit," Anne said.

"I hope no issues?" Stanley asked.

"It's the same issue of Mom refusing to accept Eddie's choice of a wife. We went over to see Flora, just to reassure her once again. You know her only crime is being Hawaiian. Hahaha!" Anne laughed out loud as Stanley joined in the laughter.

"Well, we have gone past the years of parents choosing wives or husbands for their children. Since it's Flora that Eddie has chosen, your mother should respect that, though I believe that soon everything will be okay," Stanley said.

"I hope so too because I am tired of the everyday argument. It's sickening," Anne said.

"I know things will soon be fine," Stanley said.

"I need to sleep, my dear. I'm just tired. We'll talk tomorrow," Anne said.

"Alright, goodnight," Stanley said and cut the phone. Anne dropped her phone close to the pillow and drifted off to sleep.

****

"Good morning, Eddie," Anne greeted as she saw her brother coming out of his room.

"Yea, good morning to you, Anne. Hope you slept well?" Eddie asked.

"Yes, dear," Anne replied and continued with what she was cleaning.

"What do you want me to prepare for breakfast?" Anne asked.

"Anything nice because I will be leaving for work soon to come back earlier so Flora and I can visit her parents today to choose the wedding date," Eddie said as a matter of fact.

"That's nice, great news. I've always known you to be very courageous," Anne said, smiling.

"Has Stanley said anything yet concerning your wedding?" Eddie asked.

"Yes, he will be coming back tomorrow or probably next. Whenever we have everything arranged then we can schedule the wedding date," Anne cheerfully announced.

"Good one. So, when are you going back home? Would I still meet with you?" Eddie asked.

"Well, it depends on when you're going to get back home," Anne responded.

"I will be home before 2 p.m., before leaving for Flora's house," Eddie said.

"Alright, in that case, I'll still be here," Anne said and moved towards the kitchen to prepare breakfast. When she finished eating, she dished out her brother's food and kept it on the dining table while taking hers to the room to eat. Eddie came out of the room, fully dressed as he sat down and ate his breakfast quietly. When he finished his food, he took the dishes back into the kitchen and walked to Anne's room.

"Are you leaving?" Anne asked as Eddie opened the door.

"Yes, when you finish eating, you lock the door and do take care of yourself," Eddie said.

"Alright, brother," Anne said as Eddie walked out of the house. He entered his vehicle, ignited the engine, and drove off to work. But from there, he changed his mind instead and went straight to Flora's place. When he got to the gate, he pressed the car horn to inform her that he was waiting and in less than 5 minutes, she came out of the house and entered the car.

"You look beautiful," Eddie complimented.

"Thanks, my darling," Flora replied, smiling as she put on her seat belt.

Eddie reversed his car as he drove off. Flora was all smiles throughout the journey. When they arrived at her parents' place, they discussed a few other things before delving into the wedding date issue. We scheduled it for the 1st of May, and afterward, Eddie indicated it was time for them to leave. They bade goodbye to them as Flora took turns in hugging her parents.

"Your parents are nice and super friendly, though I've always known from the first day I met them, unlike what my mom has become of late," Eddie observed.

"Your mother is still nice, it's just that I am not Chinese," Flora gently countered.

"That isn't nice. My mother's love is biased. Your parents accepted me fully, but my mom can't do the same. I hope she changes soon." Eddie said.

"I hope so too, and about Anne, sorry I didn't ask about her since morning. I was carried away by the euphoria of what we did. Has she gone home or is she still around?" Flora asked.

"Yes, she is still around, but she will be going back home today. Stanley should be coming back today or tomorrow," Eddie replied.

"Who is Stanley?" Flora asked.

"Oh sorry, I didn't tell you. I thought I did. Stanley is Anne's fiancé, and by the look of things, I think their wedding will take place before ours," Eddie replied.

"That's lovely. It means two weddings are taking place in the family, almost at the same time," Flora said, smiling.

"Yes, I just can't wait to have you as my wife," Eddie said, glancing at Flora as he accelerated the car over the posted speed limit towards Flora's house.

"And you as my husband, my soulmate, my better half," Flora responded glowingly.

Eddie smiled and as he kept his focus on the road. He wanted to get home before 2 p.m. so Anne could leave early.

Eddie pulled up at Flora's gate. A she came down from the car and bade him goodbye, Eddie drove off immediately back home. In less than thirty minutes, he got home. After he parked his vehicle, he walked inside slowly. He was exhausted after the long drive and needed to rest.

Anne was sitting comfortably on the sofa knitting when she heard a knock at the door. She stood up, peeped through the hole, and saw it was Eddie. She made haste to unlock the door and held it wide open. Eddie walked inside and sat on the couch. "Good afternoon," Anne greeted.

"Yea, same to you, dear. Can I get a glass of water, please?" Eddie requested, almost gasping for breath. It was a hot afternoon. Anne left to go into the kitchen, coming back a few minutes later and handing over the glass of water to her brother as he gulped it down in seconds. He handed the empty glass back to her.

"Thank you," he muttered.

Anne walked back to the kitchen, put the glass down, and came out.

"You looked so stressed up," Anne observed as she sat down close to her brother.

"Yes, I am," Eddie replied.

"It's expected on a hot afternoon and the long drive. So, how did it go?" Anne asked.

"Well, it went well. The wedding date has been fixed for the 1st of May. I have to get things ready before then and send out the invitation to friends and families," Eddie said.

"That's nice. I can't wait to share the news with Mom once I get home. Or rather, I think you would be the one to tell her," Anne said.

"Yeah, I will tell her myself. I wish Mom can be like Flora's parents. They were so nice and accommodating. They've never treated me as an alien. I have always felt like I was one of them," Eddie said.

"Maybe when she gets to hear that the wedding date has been fixed, hopefully, she will have no other option than to accept your choice," Anne said.

"Do you think she will let things be and accept her?" Eddie asked.

"I hope so. The wedding date is almost here so there isn't anything Mom can do about it anymore," Anne said.

"Yea, exactly," Eddie said, contented and at peace with his decision.

"I prepared something for you to eat this afternoon and later in the evening. Stanley called, and he is on his way home. He will be coming to see Mom and Dad tomorrow morning," Anne said.

"That's nice, which means you will be leaving soon, I guess," Eddie said.

"For sure. I already got my things ready," Anne said, standing up as she wandered into the guest room, coming back a few minutes later clutching her bag.

"I am good to go," Anne announced, smiling.

Eddie dipped his hands inside his pocket, brought out some money, and counted it before handing it over to Anne.

"That's for you. When I come to inform Mom and Dad of my date, I'll get some stuff for them," Eddie said.

"Alright, thanks. So, won't you drop me off?" Anne asked.

"I'd love to, but right now I'm so tired. I promise I will make it up to you some other day. The money is more than enough for your transportation. Use the excess for whatever you want, and thanks for cooking for me. You just saved me the stress," Eddie said.

"That's not a problem. Whatever I can do for my brother, I'm more than willing to do so," Anne said as she hugged her brother and walked out of the house. Eddie followed her behind to lock up the doors.

Once outside, Anne preferred to stroll down the street to the junction. She could get a ride but she saw a taxi and flagged it down as soon as she got to the intersection. She gave the driver her location as she entered and the vehicle zoomed off. Anne got home by 6 p.m. due to the traffic on the road. She met her father at the balcony reading the evening newspaper and ran to hug him.

"Good evening, Papa," Anne said happily.

"And you didn't even tell me you were not coming back home yesterday," Matt said.

"I only wanted to see Eddie since it's been quite some time. Aunty Janet was visiting him so I decided to use that opportunity to visit him, too," Anne said.

"How is Eddie doing?" Matt asked.

"He is doing great, and his future wife is doing great too, though you didn't ask about her," Anne mildly chided her dad.

"I forgot, dear," Matt said, smiling. A genial man he was.

"Which future wife are you talking about?" It was Mrs. Kate as she came out to join them at the balcony.

"Have you been eavesdropping on our conversation?" Anne asked.

"Young lady, answer my question. Which future wife are we talking about here?" Mrs. Kate insisted.

"You know who I'm talking about, of course. What's wrong with what I said?" Anne countered, flaring up a bit.

"Everything is wrong because my Ed won't marry that Hawaiian girl," Mrs. Kate said.

"That's so unfair, Mom, and you want someone else to marry your son," Anne chided.

"Will you shut up your mouth! What do you even know about marriage?" Mrs. Kate shrilled at Anne.

"I might be young, but I am not stupid and naive, Mom. Flora and Eddie love each other. That's all that matters. Why can't you just let them be? You have enjoyed yours, allow them theirs. You can't make choices for Eddie, you know. He is old enough to decide who and what he wants. You better accept that real soon," Anne said.

Eddie can't get married to Flora, not under my watch," Mrs. Kate said.

"And why can't they get married?" Matt chimed in.

"Because she isn't and will never be part of us, no matter how she tries," Mrs. Kate said.

"Is that all?" Matt asked.

"Yes!!" Mrs. Kate yelled with obvious disdain for her husband.

"That's hilarious. They love each other so why are you trying to put them asunder?" Matt asked.

"They don't love each other. Flora is only using my son, as all Hawaiians do," Mrs. Kate said.

"Can you hear yourself, Kate? Your son said he is in love with this girl Flora and even Anne confirmed that they both love each other. They are happy together and they have chosen each other. Why are you trying to ruin their lives by separating them because of nationality? Love found them, so let them be," Matt bellowed.

"They can't and won't end up with each other," Mrs. Kate said fuming.

"How sure are you?" Anne asked, smiling.

"Because I am Ed's mother, and I can't make the wrong decision for him," Mrs. Kate said.

"But he doesn't need you to decide for him, he already made the decision long ago before you came into the picture. So why do you have so much faith that Eddie will leave the girl of his dreams? Is it because you don't like her and because she is Hawaiian?" Matt asked.

"What Dad said is right. Eddie doesn't need your decision. He has made his own decision and you need to respect that. All you need to do is attend the wedding like the good mother you're supposed to be. Stop trying to mess up things for both of them," Anne chided.

"Eddie can't fix any wedding date without my permission," Mrs. Kate fired.

"You're his mother, that's accurate. But that you will decide on how he will run his life is not tenable anywhere, anymore, in this age. I hope you know that your son is now a man and he can do things all by himself?" Anne said, standing up.

"Dad, I need to rest, and lest I forget, Stanley is already back. He will be coming to the house tomorrow," Anne added as she walked into the house carrying her bag with her.

Mrs. Kate, who sat opposite her husband, shouted after Anne: "Ed can't set any wedding date without my permission. Do you get that, right?"

Matt looked at her and smiled.

"Why are you smiling?" Mrs. Kate asked.

"You haven't realized that your son is now a man and no longer a boy that you can control," Matt said and stood up and walked into the house, leaving Mrs. Kate all alone.

Anne walked into her room, shut the door. She hurriedly took her bath, wore her nightwear, and went straight to bed. She wasn't hungry and her mother's arrogant and stubborn attitude towards Flora was becoming something of a headache to her. She laid down on the bed and soon after drifted off to sleep.

The alarm clock woke Anne up from the bed as she turned to her side. She was fast enough to tap the clock to stop it from producing any other funny noise, which could have further disturbed her sleep. She then checked the time to find out it was 7 a.m. as she drew the blanket closer to her chest and shut her eyes again.

Anne's eyes flipped open as she noticed that someone was banging at the door.

"Anne, wake up! It's already 10 a.m., and you're still in bed," Mrs. Kate was shouting and banging on the door at the same time. Anne stood up slowly and walked into the bathroom to wash her face. She came out shortly afterward and opened the door.

"Good morning, Mom," she greeted.

"It's 10 a.m., and you are still in bed," Mrs. Kate charged.

"I'm sorry, Mom, just that I am so tired," Anne apologized as she went straight for the kitchen to begin doing the chores and cooking. When she finished, she went into her room to take her bath and immediately came out of the bathroom. Stanley called to inform her that he was close to the house with his parents. Anne had to wear her favorite dress as she walked outside to welcome them.

Mrs. Kate was super excited when she came out to meet Stanley and his parents. They exchanged pleasantries and talked about the wedding. By and by, the marriage is on the 21st of March. When Stanley and his parents left, Anne walked into her room feeling happy and excited. Then she noticed that her phone rang.

"Good afternoon, Eddie," Anne greeted as she picked up the phone.

"You didn't bother to call me since yesterday," Eddie charged, relatively lightly.

"I am sorry. Mom pissed me off yesterday so I had to go to bed early. This morning, I had to prepare myself because Stanley and his parents would be coming today. They just left the house now."

"Wow! That's great. I hope everything has been finalized by now," Eddie said.

"Yes, and the wedding is set for the 21st of March," Anne said, smiling.

"My baby sister is finally getting married! That's a few weeks from now," Eddie said.

"Yes, it is, and I am super excited. So, when are you coming home to tell Mom and Dad about the latest development?" Anne asked.

"Soon, dear. And as for Mom, please, you should have gotten used to her by now," Eddie said.

"So, how is Flora doing and any preparation so far concerning your wedding?" Anne asked.

"Yes, Flora has started preparation in earnest since yesterday, but soon I will join in with the necessary preparation too," Eddie said.

"That's nice," Anne said.

"Hope Mom was nice to Stanley and his family? You know she has issues with people who aren't from our tribe, and I don't know why," Eddie said, laughing.

"She was nice to them and Stanley is Chinese. Mom was super excited when she met him and she was thrilled," Anne said, smiling.

"That's nice, at least she won't disturb you or say anything. So, you're good to go. You have passed her exams," Eddie said, laughing.

"I think I have," Anne replied.

"I will talk to you later, and Flora said she should say hello to you whenever we speak on the phone. She wanted to talk to you later that evening and I told her you've already left," Eddie said.

"Alright, take care of yourself, Eddie," Anne said.

"And you too," as Eddie ended the call.

Anne dropped her phone close to the pillow as she picked up her novel lying on the dresser to read.

CHAPTER THREE

"This is outrageous. Are you saying you won't attend my wedding because Flora isn't Chinese? So be it then," Eddie said.

Eddie had traveled down home to tell his parents about the date for his wedding but his mom won't just agree as she was still persistent on having her way.

"I just can't believe this. It is not right, Kate. You mean you are determined to take it to this extent?" Matt asked.

"It's my choice. I choose to attend any occasion I wish to. If Ed were getting married to someone else, I would have graced the occasion but since he is getting married to Flora, count me out of it. I am not in support of the marriage, so I won't attend it," Mrs. Kate replied.

"Why are you doing this to yourself, Mom? Why should you allow bitterness cloud your sense of reasoning? Well, you wouldn't respect my choice but I would yours. I accept your decision, but it won't stop me from getting married to Flora," Eddie told his mom.

"She should have walked away when it was clear I didn't like her but she stayed behind. And it's clear she wants to separate you from me," Mrs. Kate said, bursting out crying. But Eddie completely ignored her, knowing full well it was a manipulative cry.

"Your daughter-in-law is one of the most beautiful souls you can ever know. You only need to calm down and get to know her well. You're only walking on the assumption that all Hawaiians are evil but you should know that it's not true, just as all Chinese are not good, either," Eddie calmly said.

"Never! I won't accept her. I don't want her, and nothing you say will make me change my mind about it," Mrs. Kate insisted.

"Even if you don't like her, it's okay. But won't you come to your son's wedding, just for his sake?" Matt chimed in.

"If you're getting married to someone else, Eddie, I would be there. But since she is a Hawaiian girl, count me out of it because you will never see me there," Mrs. Kate said.

"Your two children are about to get married and you're bitter about one marriage. Can't you see that it's so not fair, Kate? Your children's happiness should be your top priority. If Eddie has found love and happiness in Flora, why can't you just accept it and go with the flow?" Matt asked.

"Never, not with Flora," Mrs. Kate remained adamant as she stood up and walked out on them.

"How am I even sure that she is going to attend my wedding?" Anne said with a sad countenance.

"She will attend yours, that's not an issue here," Eddie said, almost angrily.

"There's no problem with that, Anne. Your Mom will attend your wedding," Matt said, smiling.

"Thanks, Dad, but what about Eddie? Will he still go ahead with the wedding?" Anne asked amidst teary eyes.

"Of course, I am going ahead with my event. I have taken time to plead with Mom and she is not budging. I'll go on with my wedding plans. She can't stop it, sure," Eddie said.

"I will still talk to your mother and hopefully, she would have a change of mind before that day," Matt assured.

"Thanks, Dad. I should be heading home now," Eddie said, standing up.

"Have a safe trip," Anne said, hugging Eddie.

Eddie quietly walked out of the building and entered the car, shutting the door angrily. He took his phone and dialed Flora's number.

"Good afternoon, sweetie. How are you doing?" Flora asked as soon as she picked the call.

"I'm okay," Eddie asked.

Flora took cognizance of Eddie's voice tone and knew that all wasn't well.

"What's the problem?" she asked.

"Hahaha!" Eddie managed a burst of wry laughter.

"Who else, but Mom," he continued almost immediately.

"She just told me now that she won't be attending our wedding. I went to give them the date for our wedding and she came up with not wanting to go. Dad and Anne tried talking to her but it all fell on deaf ears, and she walked out on us," Eddie added, clearly agitated.

"This is bad," Flora said as Eddie started hearing a couple of sobs from the background, and he knew she was crying.

"Why are you crying, darling?" Eddie asked with a heavy tinge of emotion in his voice.

"I'm just sad over what's happening. Your mom doesn't like me and now she won't even come to the wedding. I can't believe all these are happening just because I am Hawaiian. I can't even imagine the reason for the prejudice," Flora commented, still sobbing.

"Everyone is entitled to his or her opinion but that shouldn't disturb you," Eddie assured.

"Does that mean the wedding won't be held since your mom is not coming?" Flora asked.

"Who said so?" Eddie asked, raising his voice an octave.

"Your mom. Of course, her absence will send a signal to the guests and so I think we should postpone this wedding until we get her consent," Flora pleaded.

"Nothing is going to change the date except death. Our wedding will still go on. Don't worry about that, okay? And stop thinking about it." Eddie added.

"I'll try not to. It's disconcerting and it's draining me," Flora said.

"I will call you when I get home. Take care of yourself," Eddie said.

"You too. Drive safe, my love," Flora responded and ended the call.

Eddie dropped the phone and drove off straight to his aunt's place, hoping that maybe somehow, she would be able to talk to his mom, just for Flora's sake. In a few minutes, he arrived at Mrs. Janet's, stepping down from the car and shutting the door behind him. Mrs. Janet was sitting comfortably on the balcony when she saw Eddie walk up to her and greeted her.

"Eddie, you didn't tell me you were coming," she remarked with a wry smile.

"Even if I got here and you weren't home, I would have waited for you to come home. That's how serious what brought me here is," Eddie said as he sat down abruptly beside her.

"What's the problem, young man? You don't look happy at all. I hope it's not about your mom again?" she asked, looking him in the eyes.

Eddie was quiet from what seemed an eternity. He was reflective, uncertain, and angry. But after what seemed a long time, Eddie opened up to Mrs. Janet.

"Aunty, we have set our wedding for the 1st of May," Eddie began.

"That's lovely. Congratulations! Is that why you are angry?" Mrs. Janet remarked again.

"No, of course. It's Mom, your sister. She said she wouldn't be there. And of course, you already know the reason. Flora committed a crime for being a Hawaiian," Eddie blurted out.

Mrs. Janet was quiet, entirely at a loss of what to say. She bowed her head and became engrossed in thoughts. Anne never knew that Mrs. Kate could take this issue this far by refusing to be at her son's wedding. She became disturbed.

"I have talked to her. Dad has tried too and even Anne, but she won't budge. That's why I'm here too, apart from informing you personally of my date," Eddie added as she waited on Mrs. Janet to speak.

"I don't know what's wrong with my sister, but I will try and talk to her." That was all Mrs. Janet managed to say as she looked up.

"But whatever it is that has made my sister become so biased against a certain people is not right," she added.

"Please, Aunty, help talk to her too, at least for Flora's peace of mind. But if she disagrees, I will still go ahead with the wedding, as I don't know what else to do about my mother. I've explored every possible avenue," Eddie said.

"Don't worry, things will end well. I know so. You look hungry, have you had anything to eat?" Mrs. Janet asked.

"Not yet. I left home with anger. I couldn't taste anything," Eddie replied.

"You wait here while I get something for you to eat, okay?" Mrs. Janet said as she stood up.

"Thanks, Aunty," Eddie said, smiling for the first time since he came into Mrs. Janet's home, an expression that didn't escape her notice.

"Ahaa! My boy is happy again. You know I love that smile of yours," Mrs. Janet noted as she dashed off to the kitchen, reappearing moments after with a bowl of rice. Eddie ate in silence. When he finished eating, she took the tray inside and came out shortly.

"Is Anne at home?" Mrs. Janet asked as she came out of the kitchen.

"I won't say yes because I am not sure, though she was at home when I left. I doubt if she would still be there as she said something like going out to see someone. You know her wedding is in a few days, and she is preparing for it," Eddie answered.

"Call Anne on the phone," Mrs. Janet said.

Eddie took out his phone and dialed Anne's number. She immediately picked up.

"Anne, are you at home?" Mrs. Janet asked.

"I left a few minutes ago after the decorator called me. I will be home later in the evening," Anne said.

"Oh, okay," Eddie said.

"Is there any problem?" Anne asked.

"Not to worry, okay?" Eddie said and ended the call.

"She isn't at home, Aunty," Eddie said.

"I wanted her to pass the phone to Kate but not to worry. I will talk to her when I see her at Anne's wedding," Mrs. Janet said.

"Alright, Aunty. I should get going now, and thanks for the food," Eddie said, smiling.

"You're welcome," Mrs. Janet said.

Eddie stood up and walked to where he parked his car and drove back home, totally immersed in his thoughts.

The days turned into weeks and it was the 21st of March, Anne's wedding day. Anne looked so beautiful in her gown with scanty patches of makeup on her face. She had always preferred light makeup. Anne was in her father's house, where every other family member was expected to gather before going to the church. As soon as she stepped out of her room with her maid of honor, she met her mother chit-chatting with Mrs. Janet as they stood in the sitting room.

"You're looking magnificent," Mrs. Kate, her mom, observed as she admired her daughter.

"Thanks, Mama," Anne said, smiling. She was still smiling when the door opened as Eddie and Flora walked in.

"Hmmm! The elegant Anne. You're looking wonderful," Mrs. Janet said to Anne, smiling broadly.

"Thanks, Aunty." Anne acknowledged.

"And I can't even recognize her anymore," Flora chipped in as she and Eddie drew nearer to where Anne stood with Mrs. Kate and Mrs. Janet.

"Thanks so much, dear," Anne replied Flora, brimming with smiles.

"Be happy little Sis, it's your day," Eddie offered.

"Sure, brother," Anne replied.

"Good morning, ma'am," Flora greeted Mrs. Kate and Mrs. Janet with a broad grin on her face.

"And what is she doing here? Was she invited?" Mrs. Kate shot at Flora.

"Sorry, Mom. Who are you talking to?" Anne asked, clearly embarrassed.

"Eddie, this is a family affair. Why would you bring your concubine here?" Mrs. Kate continued her onslaught against Flora.

"And who are you referring to as my concubine?" Eddie asked, getting upset, his eyes glaring.

"Mom, can you stop this? Why are you trying to ruin my day when it has not even started?" Anne said, blushing all over her face, with goose pimples running through her skin.

"I will be waiting in the car," Flora said amidst tears as she stormed out of the room.

"Are you serious, Mom? Flora is a girl, just like your daughter. She left her place of abode to come here to celebrate with me and you just made her cry. Why? You have completely lost it, I must say. What's happening to you?" Anne asked, gesticulating widely, very angry at her mother.

"It's so not fair, Kate! Does she look like a concubine? That's your son's wife-to- be. When will you accept that?" Mrs. Janet angrily came in.

"I won't, and I will never accept that," Mrs. Kate yelled at her sister.

"Then fine, keep assuming that I will stop my marriage because you don't like my woman. You treat her bad, call her names, say whatever you want, but the truth is, she is going to be my wife, and you can't even change that. If it weren't Anne's day, I would have walked out of this house and you won't see me again. You already made it clear that you won't be there on my wedding day so I am not bothered. Flora is my choice, she is! Flora has loved you how a child would love a mother but instead, what did you give to her? Pain and that's wickedness," Eddie shrilled at her mother as he went after Flora.

"I won't stop until she realizes she is not wanted in this family. Even if you're married, I'm going to make life unbearable for her until she leaves," Mrs. Kate yelled after Eddie.

"Everybody wants her except you," Matt said as he came into the sitting room.

"You're the only one bitter about their union yet you don't have any reason to be so. Do you think you can change a man's resolve with your silly attitude?" Matt continued.

"And Kate, moreover, I heard you said you wouldn't be there on your son's wedding day. I wanted to talk to you about it today but it seems you already have your mind made up by your display just now. Of course, you can be sure that the wedding will go on with or without your presence and stop dreaming that Eddie will wake up one morning and leave Flora. My dear sister, that dream won't happen. It's only going to play in your head. You just don't know what you're doing," Mrs. Janet said, still angry at Mrs. Kate.

"Now you have gotten what you wanted," Anne said, sighing heavily.

Eddie met Flora inside the car, sobbing as he tried to console her.

"You have been crying, right?" Eddie asked as he tenderly held her hand.

"It's okay for you to cry. What Mom said in there hurts a lot but don't worry as she won't say that to you anymore henceforth," Eddie assured.

"Why does she hate me so much when I have done nothing to her, other than who I am.? I just want her to see me as a daughter. I want her to love me. I love her, and I care about her, but she just hates me, treating me with disdain," Flora said in between heavy sobs.

"Don't worry about my Mom. I am telling you this, it's a promise and will be the last time she will say this to you," Eddie said as he cleaned up the tears that were dripping down Flora's cheeks. He hugged her, a hug of assurance, and it made her smile.

"My armored knight. It's okay. Let's go back inside," Flora said.

"We will stay here till it's time to leave for church, then we can go with them," Eddie said.

After a few minutes, they all drove to the church, and the wedding began. Flora and Eddie quietly walked inside. When the whole event was over, and as people were giving the couple their gifts, Flora was the last to drop her gift for them. Eddie whispered something into Anne's ear before he and Flora left for home. Eddie dropped Flora at her place after meandering through the heavy traffic and then he went back home.

As Eddie went inside, he hurriedly had his bath, and as he came out, he retired to the bedroom and was about to drift off to sleep when his ringing tone alerted him. He checked who the caller was and discovered it was his sister. He swiped and received the call.

"Anne, how are you doing?" Eddie asked.

"I am fine. Are you sleeping already?" Anne asked.

"Almost. Any problem?" Eddie asked.

"I am just sorry about what happened today. I am sorry, you know it. I don't have Flora's number. I would have called to apologize to her directly. What mom said hurts like hell, and if I were the one, I would have cried myself to stupor. Please forgive mom," Anne apologized.

"Can you send me Flora's number so I can call and apologize to her myself?" she added.

"Alright, no problem," Eddie said and ended the call as he sent Flora's number to Anne.

"What's the problem?" Stanley, who sat on the hotel bed where they had gone for their honeymoon, asked.

"It's my mom. She insulted Flora when she came to the house with Eddie to see me. I just can't imagine the kind of pain she went through when Mom uttered those words to her," Anne further offered.

"What did she say?" Stanley asked.

"She called Flora a concubine in a very demeaning manner, even when she is fully aware that they are getting married soon," Anne said.

"That's saddening, very humiliating," Stanley said.

"Oh, her number just came in now," Anne said as she dialed Flora's number.

"Good evening Flora. It's me, Anne."

"Oh, Anne, the latest wife in town. How are you doing?" Flora asked.

"I am doing great," Anne said.

"Sorry I didn't stay for the after-wedding bash. I had to leave with Eddie. Hope it went well?" Flora apologized.

"I understand, it was because of Mom. And I am sorry about what she said to you earlier today. Please just forget it and forgive her. Trust me, one day, she will see you as a daughter." Anne said.

"I was furious in the morning when it happened but I am okay now. I understand why Mom said all that to me. You don't need to worry," Flora said.

"Alright, thank you for your understanding. You have a beautiful heart of gold," Anne said, smiling.

"Thank you. Happy married life, dear," Flora said.

"Thanks, dear. I will get to say that to you very soon," Anne said.

"Yea. Sure. Take care," Flora said and ended the call.

"Guess she is okay now," Stanley said.

"Oh yes, such a beautiful soul," Anne responded gleefully, as she laid back on the bed and slept beside her husband.

****

Six weeks passed and it was Eddie's wedding day. Everyone was super excited except for Mrs. Kate. Matt was having a hard time convincing Mrs. Kate to dress up so she would attend the wedding, but it all fell on deaf ears. Eddie arrived together with Mrs. Janet while Anne and Stanley followed in tow as they were talking.

"Oh, thank God you're here," Matt said as soon as he saw his children.

"What's the problem?" Anne asked.

"Your mom is insistent on what she said that she won't be at the wedding," Matt offered.

"Good morning, Eddie," Anne greeted as Stanley gripped hands with him.

"Why are you all here? I already made it clear at the beginning that I'm not in support of this marriage so that I won't be attending the wedding," Mrs. Kate said.

"And that sounds nice to you, huh!? Even your own son's wedding? I thought that by now, you must have had a change of mind. What happened to you, sister?" Mrs. Janet asked.

"I pleaded that I didn't like this girl and the least I expected Ed to do was to leave her and find a better girl, but what did he do? He went ahead and set a date for the wedding without even involving me. Now you expect me to be there? That's not going to happen," Mrs. Kate remained indignant.

"To dump Flora just because of your unfounded bias? Are you aware we are talking about emotions here? Do you just dump people out of your life like that? Mama! It isn't fair. Even if you have issues with Flora's ancestry, at least attend the wedding because of your son. It's his day," Anne, half pleaded.

"I am not stepping an inch out of here," Mrs. Kate said.

"Alright, no problem. I don't see any reason why anyone should be pleading with Mom. She has already made up her mind and we have to accept and respect that," Eddie said.

"Dad, please dress up so we can start going," Eddie curtly said as he turned to his father.

"You see, that witch has turned the face of my son against me," Mrs. Kate said and started weeping, but Eddie ignored her. "What else exactly do you want? I am not you but were I to be so, I'll simply dress up and follow us and then watch the marriage unfold. But since you are still insisting that you won't be there, then no problem at all," Anne angrily said and left the room.

Shortly after Matt was ready and came out of his room, he joined the rest of the family members in the sitting room. He went to his son, held his hands, and gripped them firmly. Without uttering any word to him, and turning to his wife, he said, "Take care of the house." Matt said and walked out with the rest of the family, leaving Mrs. Kate all alone in the house. "I didn't grow up with this person. I wish my sister's old self will resurface," Mrs. Janet said as she was leaving the house with others.

When they got to the wedding venue, no one noticed the absence of Mrs. Kate. Everything went well. Flora looked just stunning that day. Eddie kept telling her how lucky he was soon to be married to her. When the event ended, another car, a cabman Eddie hired, took Anne, Mrs. Janet, and Matt while Eddie drove his wife home. He didn't opt for any hotel. He wanted to start his marital life straight away from home.

The cabman took Mrs. Janet to her house before heading to Matt's residence, where he dropped him and Anne. Anne was full of smiles as they entered the house. She was happy that the wedding was successful, even with the absence of her mom. As she and Matt walked inside, they met Mrs. Kate sitting alone on the couch, just staring into emptiness, while knitting.

"Good evening, Mama," Anne greeted as she sat down abruptly beside her mother.

"What are you doing here?" Mrs. Kate yelled.

"Mom, this is still my house. Can't I come around and stay here, even for a month if I wanted to? Come on, Mom!" Anne said.

"Leave her alone, this is her father's house," Matt said. Mrs. Kate looked at both of them and kept quiet. She continued with what she was knitting.

"Can you give me that once you have finished? It's going to be very beautiful. The color combination is just wow!" Anne said, trying hard to cheer her mom up, seeing how downcast she looked.

Mrs. Kate acted like she didn't hear her.

"Dad, are you okay, or do you want anything for dinner?" Anne turned to her father.

"I am okay. It was a sumptuous meal we had at the wedding. I will just have my bath and then rest a little bit," Matt replied as he stood up and walked straight to his room.

"Mom, you missed a lot. The wedding was fabulous. Flora looked like an angel straight from heaven. Mom, when Flora came to my wedding, did you take time to look at her very well? She looks Chinese. Had you been there at the wedding today, you would have noticed what I was telling you. Flora is either Chinese or maybe she has Chinese ancestry in her veins," Anne said.

"How did you know?" Mrs. Kate asked, looking up for the first time since Anne and Matt came into the house, her eyes lighting up in hope.

"Now you're interested in the conversation. Hahaha! Momma. Although I didn't ask her, she sure looks like one. I can bet my life on that," Anne said and stood up.

"Well, if she is not, she is not. She might be married to Eddie but that doesn't mean she has been accepted into this family. She has no place here," Mrs. Kate said.

"You're the only one who didn't accept her. Mom, speak for yourself only. Everyone else accepts her, and besides, Eddie loves her dearly. Relatives far and wide all support the marriage. You are alone in this," Anne said and walked into her room. She quickly had her bath and changed into her nightwear. Then she laid down on the bed and called her husband, Stanley.

"Hi, darling!" Stanley exclaimed on hearing her voice.

"Good evening, my love. I would have called earlier but we just got back home a few minutes ago," Anne said.

"That's not a problem, but I hope you explained to Eddie why I wasn't able to come?" Stanley said.

"Oh, yes, I did. Eddie understands," Anne said.

"You need to go to bed now and have your rest. It must have been a hectic day for you. I can only imagine how busy you were all day attending to guests. We will talk tomorrow," Stanley said. "Yea. Goodnight dear and take care," Anne said.

"And you too," Stanley replied.

Anne switched off her phone and as she placed it on her dresser, she laid on the bed and covered herself up properly with the blanket.

The next morning Anne woke up early and helped her mom with sundry chores. Afterwards, she prepared breakfast. Then Anne dished out her own and ate quietly. When she finished eating, she took the plates into the kitchen and washed them. Then Anne went back into her room to sleep. Anne woke up later by 11 a.m., took her bath, and later got dressed in the same clothing she wore to the wedding. Anne came out and met her mom and dad, eating in the dining room.

"I can see you're enjoying your breakfast," Anne said, leaning on the wall.

"This food tastes nice," Matt said, smiling.

"Good morning, Mama and Papa," Anne greeted.

"Why are you all dressed up already? Are you going somewhere?" Mrs. Kate asked in between munching on her food.

"Oh, yes. I am going back home," Anne replied.

"Oh! I thought you would be spending the weekend with us?" Matt asked.

"Mom won't allow me," Anne said, eyeing her mom, smiling.

"I never said that," Mrs. Kate protested.

"But you said so last night when I was going into my room. Apart from that, I need to go back to my husband," Anne said.

"Alright. Go well, my daughter," Matt said.

Anne went back inside her room and came out, clutching her bag with her. She hugged her mom and dad before leaving the house. The taxi that Anne had ordered was already outside waiting for her. She entered the car and the driver zoomed off.

Anne got home at around 1 p.m. Her husband had already left for work. She kept her bag in the room, took her time, and arranged the room properly, as she had left it unkempt. The dirty clothes were washed and hung out to dry while she cleaned up the sitting room and the balcony chairs before heading to the kitchen. She then arranged everywhere and took time to mop the floor. After which, she prepared lunch and dinner at the same time so she won't have to enter the kitchen again. After dishing out a plate for herself, Anne ate slowly while watching a series on the television. When she finished eating, she washed her plate and went straight to her room to bathe again. When Anne finished, she quickly laid on the bed to recover her lost strength and didn't know when she drifted off to sleep.

"Wake up!"

Anne opened her eyes slowly to see it was Stanley standing over her.

"Good afternoon." she greeted.

"It's evening, my dear. I'm back from work," Stanley gently corrected, smiling and stretching his hand toward her as she firmly gripped, getting up from the bed and walked into the bathroom to wash her eyes. She came out a few minutes later and sat on the bed while Stanley was busy removing his clothes.

"How was work today?" Anne asked.

"It was exciting, as usual. You look stressed," Stanley observed.

"Don't worry, I am fine. Do you want to eat now?" Anne asked.

"I need to bathe first before dinner," Stanley replied.

"Alright, when you're through, you come to the dining table," Anne said and walked out. She went straight to the kitchen to warm the food and she dished out for herself and Stanley. Anne kept them at the dining table while going back to get water to drink. By the time she returned to the dining room, Stanley was already sitting on the dining chair.

"This food looks appetizing," Stanley said, smiling.

"Thanks, dear," Anne replied as she carried the glasses of water in her hand. She took her seat beside her husband as they both ate quietly. When they finished eating their food, Anne cleared the table and washed the dishes before returning to the sitting room. He sat close to her husband and rested her head on his broad shoulders. There was a live football game showing on the TV that held Stanley's full attention. Outside it was dark already.

Horns from various vehicles were blaring as loud music was playing in a nearby club. Anne was quiet, not knowing when to start up a conversation with Stanley as all his attention was on the football match showing on the TV. But her chance to talk came when it was half time for the game.

"Can I ask a question?" Anne said as soon as the referee blew the half time whistle.

"Sure, you can," Stanley said while playing with some loose strands of hair on Anne's head.

"When are we going to start to have a family? Eddie is married, the same as my other older sisters. I would want my children to start playing with their cousins as soon as possible," Anne said.

"We will have children soon. I just need to pay off the loan I took from Dad for the house down payment so we can move out of here. I mean, I am not comfortable with this noisy environment. Once that is complete, then we will start thinking of having children," Stanley replied.

"That should be in a few months, right?" Anne asked.

"Yes, maybe years, but it won't be long," Stanley assured her. Anne lifted her head from his husband's lap and looked at him, searching for muted answers in his eyes.

"Did you say years?" She finally said, looking surprised.

"Oh, yes. Are you angry?" Stanley asked.

"Of course, I am angry. It sounds weird. How can I continue taking contraceptives for years? A married woman like me? I just want to know what it feels like to be a mother and having my children playing with their cousins," Anne said.

"I promise it's going to be soon," Stanley said, firmly gripping her shoulders and kissing her forehead in the process.

"Alright. No problem. I'm going into the bedroom. I know you won't come in until the football match is over," Anne said and walked into the room without waiting for any response from her husband.

Stanley knew she was angry but he needed to settle all debts first. Stanley only wanted the best for his children. He knew he needed a bit of discipline to achieve that. A soon as the football match was over, he turned off the TV and went into the bedroom to meet his wife.

****

About ten months later, Anne sat in the sitting room, waiting for Stanley to come out from the room dressed for work so she could walk him to the car. It was a bright Monday morning when her phone rang. She picked it up after seeing it was her brother calling.

"Good morning, Eddie," Anne greeted.

"Yea, same to you, Anne. How are you doing?" Eddie asked.

"I am fine, and how is Flora?" Anne asked.

"She is doing great. She just gave birth to a baby girl this morning!" Eddie said.

"Oh, my goodness! Congratulations, brother me. I am so happy," Anne shouted excitingly, smiling.

"Thanks, dear. I just called to let you know. Send my greetings to Stanley," Eddie said.

"Alright. You can expect me soon and goodbye," Anne said. She left the sitting room and hurried into the bedroom.

"I heard your shout of excitement and was coming to check up on you," Stanley said.

"Flora just gave birth to a baby girl this morning," Anne informed Stanley.

"Wow! Just wow! That's good news. Congratulations to your brother too," Stanley said, smiling.

"Just can't wait to break the news to Mom and Dad, though I know Eddie must have informed them. Can I go back home right away? I will come back the day after tomorrow as I will need to visit Eddie and Flora to see the newborn," Anne pleaded.

"Sure, you can. Why not?" Stanley acquiesced.

"Thank you so much, darling. I already made lunch and it will be okay for dinner this evening," Anne said as she picked a few of her clothes and placed them in her bag.

"You're excited," Stanley observed. Of course, he knew his wife had always been a lover of children.

"Yes, I am. I will be back the day after tomorrow, as promised. You only need to pick any food you want to eat from the freezer and warm it up, okay?"

"I'll go with you to your office, and from there you can catch a taxi to my father's house," Anne added.

"Sure," Stanley said as he picked up his bag and headed out of the house.

After spending a few hours on the road, Anne got home as she ran inside and met her father, discussing something with her mom.

"Anne, you didn't tell anyone you are coming?" Mrs. Kate said.

"I came to pass the good news across to you both," Anne said, smiling.

"So, what's the good news?" Matt asked.

"Flora just gave birth this morning to a baby girl. Eddie called this morning to inform me," Anne replied, smiling.

"Wow! That's good news but he already told us. It was such good news. I'm happy, so happy," Mrs. Kate said, smiling.

"All the same. Congratulations to my son," Matt added.

"But Mom, I thought you don't like her," Anne asked, eyeing her mom.

"Yes, I don't, but that doesn't mean I will hate my grandchild. I can't wait to see the newest baby in the family," Mrs. Kate said, smiling.

"I will visit them tomorrow morning before I go back home.

Maybe we all can go there tomorrow morning," Anne said.

"That's a nice idea," Matt said.

"And you, Anne, when are you going to give me a grandchild? You got married before Eddie, you know," Mrs. Kate observed. Anne kept mute and looked away as her facial expression changed.

"Anne, your mother, is talking to you," Matt said.

"I will have children soon, very soon, but not this year and maybe not next year," Anne replied.

"Why is that so? Is there any issue?" Mrs. Kate asked, a bit worried.

"Stanley and I are waiting for some things to get done before we can start our own family, and very soon, I will have children," Anne replied.

"What's that?" Mrs. Kate asked.

"Mama, my husband and I just want the best for our children, and once the time is right, I will get pregnant, but for now, we need to finish up some things," Anne said.

"Well, if you and your husband are okay with whatever decision you both made, then it's fine with us," Matt said.

"If you say so, Anne. I don't have anything else to ask," Mrs. Kate said.

"Mama, I am hungry. Let me go inside and drop my bag," Anne said as she stood up and walked inside. Mrs. Kate and Matt continued with their discussion.

CHAPTER FOUR

"Good morning, sweetie." Flora greeted as she saw her husband all dressed up early in the morning.

"Good morning, dear," Eddie responded but still busy with the buttons of his shirt.

"Where are you off to this early?" Flora asked, looking surprised. He woke up when she was still asleep.

"I am going home to my parents," Eddie replied.

"Home? Really? Just like that? But it would help if you had told me since last night and I would have woken up early to prepare something for you to eat this morning. But I hope there is no problem," Flora asked.

"Anne called late in the night when you and the children were fast asleep. Dad is seriously sick and I need to rush home so I can take him to the hospital," Eddie replied as he picked up his car keys, very much in haste.

"I will follow you," Flora said, standing up.

"No, please. Just take care of the children and take them to school. When I get there, I'll alert you," Eddie said and left the bedroom immediately.

Flora knelt and said a quick prayer, standing up immediately after to make the bed and clean up the bedroom. She took her husband's clothes, coupled with her children's clothes, into the laundry room to wash them. She was still washing the clothes when her four-year-old daughter Cynthia walked up to her, smiling, fully awake.

"Good morning, Mommy," Cynthia said, still wearing her infectious smiling as she sat down on a children's chair by the corner.

"Good morning, my dear," Flora responded with a broad smile as she dried her hands. When she finished her washing and rinsing, she stood up and walked into the sitting room with her daughter.

"What of Daddy?" Cynthia asked.

"Dad has gone to visit Grandpa, but soon he will be back," Flora assured, smiling as she asked her to stay put on the chair. She walked into the children's room and discovered that the twins Christine and Christopher were still sleeping. Flora hurriedly left them and walked back to her room quickly to have her bath, and in less than a minute, she was done and rushed back to the sitting room. She found Cynthia playing with her toys. Ignoring her, Flora walked into the kitchen, prepared breakfast for them, packing their lunch in their separate bags, and took it out to the sitting room. She dished their breakfast too and kept it in the dining room to cool off a little before they could eat it. She had to bathe Cynthia first and dress her up for school while she did the same for the twins. Cynthia fed herself while Flora fed her twins since they were just two-and-a-half years old. When they finished eating, she held them by the hand as they all walked out of the house. Their taxi was already waiting for them as Flora helped her children enter the cab. As soon as she sat down, she asked the taxi man to drive off. She intended finishing up spreading the clothes once she returned from taking the children to school.

****

"What's wrong with him?" Eddie asked immediately he rushed into the house, while his father was just lying on the bed shivering.

"I don't know, and how come Anne isn't here yet?" Mrs. Kate retorted.

"I don't think she will come here. She will meet us at the hospital," Eddie offered.

"Daddy, can you hear me?" Eddie asked his father while tenderly holding his father's hands.

"I want to see Anne too. Tell her to come here please," Matt said, stifling a cough.

"But..." Eddie made to say but was cut short by Matt.

"There is no but, just do what I want," Matt insisted as Eddie took out his phone and called Anne, informing her of their father's desire, but it took forever before she finally got home because of the distance. She rushed inside the house, panting.

"Take it easy, Anne. How's your child?" Eddie asked.

"He is fine, he is with his dad," Anne said as she knelt beside her father.

"Daddy, I am here. You don't have to worry. You will be okay before you know it," She assured.

"And even if I don't get better," Matt said and coughed a bit loudly.

"Of course, you will. You have always advised that we should be positive at all times," Anne reminded him.

"I wanted to see your beautiful face, the face of my daughter," Matt said in between bouts of cough.

Mrs. Kate rushed inside to get water, returned, and handed it over to Anne, who gently gave her father the water to drink.

"You don't have you to talk, Dad. Save your strength, please. Let's take you to the hospital. From there, we would know what next to do," Anne said.

"There is no need for that, Anne. It feels better here and knowing full well that I am going to a better place," Matt said, smiling.

"What do you mean? I don't understand," Eddie came in.

"I don't understand what you are talking about, Father," Anne joined.

"Please, you all should take care of my grandchildren. They should always know that Grandpa loves them and I would have wished to stay with them for a longer time but I need to go home," Matt said faintly.

"What're all these? What are you talking about, Father?" Eddie was alarmed.

"His hands are getting cold," Anne said while standing up.

"Daddy, Daddy! Daddy!" Anne shouted, but it was silence from Matt.

Eddie held his father and kept tapping him, but he wasn't responding.

"Daddy, wake up, wake up, please," Anne shouted and became hysterical.

On hearing the shout, Mrs. Kate rushed into the room to know what the problem was. She had gone into the kitchen to prepare hot soup for the husband to take.

"Matt!" She shouted his name, but there was no reply.

At that moment, their father was dead and gone. Anne kept tapping her father and shaking his body, calling out his name, but only silence greeted her.

"Please wake up. Daddy! Daddy!" Eddie pleaded with his father as he was at the point of breaking down.

Mrs. Kate went outside and sat down on the floor quietly and kept shouting and crying such that people living close by rushed to find out what the problem was. They saw the lifeless body of Matt lie silently and peacefully on the bed, and they knew he was dead. Anne and Eddie were still in shock, yet to believe that their father had passed. Someone talked to them a few minutes ago, and now he is gone, just like that.

Eddie walked out of the room with Anne. They went to where their mom held her as more and more people were coming to the house.

"Has he woken up?" Mrs. Kate asked as Anne and Eddie held her. Eddie wavered his head in as he knelt beside his mother and cried himself to stupor. They had lost a father and a husband that very day, right in front of their eyes.

The whole family was in mourning. The death of their father, Matt, deeply saddened Mrs. Kate and her four children. Two of her daughters lived overseas with their husbands since they got married.

After the burial, Anne suggested her mom stay with her as she couldn't imagine her living in the same house where she watched her husband die before her very own eyes. Mrs. Kate had to go to live with Anne subsequently. It took her some time to accept the fact that her husband has passed away.

On a particular morning, Anne went into the room where her mother stayed with her breakfast.

"Good morning, Mama," Anne greeted.

"Good morning, my dear. How are you doing?" Mrs. Kate asked, smiling.

"I am fine," Anne replied. She knew deep down that her mom was still hurting over the demise of her husband.

"I brought you something to eat," Anne said.

"I am not hungry now, but you can put it down it. I will eat later," Mrs. Kate said as Anne caught a wave of sadness glossed over her face.

"Mom, this isn't fair. It's been months now. You have to move on. Dad is gone, and he won't be back. We all are sad about what happened but we can't question nature. Since then, you barely ate, and if you continue this way, you're going to fall ill. Please, though Dad is gone, at least your children are with you coupled with your grandchildren. How do you think they will feel if they wake up in the morning and hear that you're gone too? Stop doing this to us, Mommy," Anne pleaded as tears trickled down her cheeks.

"It's okay, Anne. Never mind. Just drop it on the table. I will eat it when I'm hungry," Mrs. Kate managed to say as she stood up and walked out of the room. She went to the balcony and sat down there, all alone. Anne decided to leave her to herself, too, thinking Mom needed to be alone for her total healing. But Mom never took her eyes off her. Anne sat in her room, observing her as she sat on the couch on the balcony. Mrs. Kate sat there thinking of her life with Matt and how she never wanted him at first. It took her years to start coming to terms and develop a level of affection for him. It dawned on her she had lived with an angel of a man without realizing it. Mom didn't know when a little girl approached her.

"Hello! Good morning, Grandma," The little girl greeted while smiling as she came closer to Mrs. Kate.

"How are you doing?" Mrs. Kate asked.

"I am fine, and you, Grandma?" the little girl asked, looking Mrs. Kate straight into the eyes, with her clear white eyes.

"I am good, thank you," Mrs. Kate said, smiling. She was surprised the little girl was feeling comfortable with her despite knowing little about her.

"Where are your parents?" Mrs. Kate asked.

"We live down the street, and my parents are at home," the girl said.

"And what's your name, little one?" Mrs. Kate asked, finding herself drawn to the girl.

"Rose," she said, smiling as she gave Mrs. Kate the sweets she was holding.

"Thank you, dear," Mrs. Kate said as she accepted the sweets from Rose.

Rose advanced closer and hugged Mrs. Kate before running away. Mrs. Kate smiled as she rose from the couch she sat on and walked straight to her room, ready to eat her food. She swallowed it slowly, smiling. Anne came in and saw her mom eating and smiling to herself. She was relieved and silently thanked God for the change she saw in her mom. She silently left the room, very happy and excited. She took her phone and dialed Eddie's number immediately as soon as she got into her room.

"Anne!" Eddie exclaimed as he picked up.

"How are you doing?" Anne asked.

"I'm okay. Sorry I haven't called for two days now. I've been working on this particular project I need to finish. How's Mom? Had she had anything to eat today?" Eddie asked.

"Oh yes, she did," Anne replied, smiling.

"I can sense the excitement in your voice. What happened?" Eddie asked.

"I don't know who that girl is, but she is a God-sent. After she talked to Mom and left, Mom came inside and ate her food without me pleading with her to eat," Anne said.

"Oh! Thank God. At least she ate something. I've been so worried about her. I will pay you, people, a visit this weekend. I need to see Mom," Eddie said.

"Alright, that's nice. Do take care of yourself. I need to take care of my baby. I'll talk to you later," Anne said.

"Alright. Goodbye," Eddie said. It was a pleasant Monday morning.

Anne woke up and wandered over to her baby's bed. She slowly carried her baby boy and fed him. She continued feeding while Anne went away to attend to some chores.

And since that Monday, no day passed without Rose paying a visit to Mrs. Kate. Rose's parents later got to know who their daughter was visiting because she was always leaving the house, claiming to see her friend. Mrs. Kate found great company in the six-year-old girl. Rose was very comfortable around Anne too, and she played with her baby boy together with Mrs. Kate.

A day came when Rose visited, but Mrs. Kate was in the bathroom so Anne asked her to sit down and wait while she went inside and came back with a glass of juice. She handed it over to Rose who took it from her with a wide grin, thanking her as well.

"So, how are your parents doing today?" Anne asked as she knelt close to her.

"They're fine," Rose said, smiling.

"Can I ask you a question?" Anne said, smiling.

"Okay," Rose said, shifting a bit on her seat.

"Why do you love playing with my mom?" Anne asked.

"She looks like my grandma, who I never got to meet," Rose replied.

"How did you know she looks like your grandma?" Anne prodded further.

"My mom showed me her picture, the picture of my grandma," Rose replied, smiling.

"Is that so?" Anne said, smiling and nodding her head in a clearer understanding of the girl's attachment to her mom.

"Drink your juice while I go check on my mom to let her know that you're here," Anne said, smiling as she stood up. Mrs. Kate, who was standing at the door all the time, heard all their conversation and smiled to herself.

"No need for that, I am here," she said as she came out from where she was leaning. Rose stood up and hugged her tightly.

"Mommy is here so I will leave you two. I need to feed my son," Anne said as she walked into the room.

Rose and Mrs. Kate walked out together and stayed at the balcony holding hands as Rose kept throwing funny questions at Mrs. Kate, who was eagerly answering all with a smile. It was clear that Rose was one of the best things that happened to her after her husband's death. The little girl was always there to cheer her up and make her happy. Anne had to take her mom's food outside for her to eat. She stood a distance away, watching her and Rose, watching as she ate and fed Rose. Soon Mrs. Kate finished the food together with Rose and beckoned to Anne to pick up the plate. Mrs. Kate had every reason to smile again.

On a Saturday morning, Eddie drove to Anne's house to see his mom. He parked his car and walked into the compound. He knocked at the door as he waited for someone to open it.

"Eddie!" Anne called and hugged him immediately, she opened the door and seeing it was her brother.

"How are you doing?" Anne asked as she released herself from his embrace.

"I am doing pretty good," Eddie said, smiling.

"I don't need to ask as I can see for myself that you're looking great. How about the children and Flora?" Anne asked.

"They are all fine and wanted to come, but I asked them to stay back. Maybe during the holidays, they will come and visit," Eddie explained.

"What about your husband?" Eddie asked.

"He went to the store to get groceries," Anne replied.

"And your baby boy, Dennis, and Mom?" Eddie asked.

"Oh, Mom is in her room and my baby is sleeping. I just fed him a few minutes ago and put him to bed." Anne answered. "Alright. Let me go and see Mom," Eddie said as he walked behind Anne to Mrs. Kate's room.

"Mom, how are you doing?" Eddie asked as soon as Anne opened the door.

On seeing Eddie, Mrs. Kate stood up and hugged him so tightly.

She had missed her son so much.

"You didn't tell me you were coming, Ed?" Mrs. Kate asked with a wide grin on her face.

"I didn't want Anne to tell you because I was upset that you haven't been eating properly, and I was worried. That's why I had come to ask you what the problem was but I'm happy that everything has changed and you're slowly moving on," Eddie said, smiling.

"Well, all thanks to Rose. That girl is an angel, and she has been of a great company to me since we first met at the balcony over there," Mrs. Kate answered, pointing to the balcony.

"She cheers me up with her innocence and presence," Mrs. Kate added.

"Mom, who is Rose? I don't understand," Eddie feigned ignorance. Of course, Anne had hinted him on that.

"Rose is the little girl that normally comes around to spend time with me," Mrs. Kate offered.

"Little girl? That sounds strange and exciting too," Eddie said. "Well, she thinks Mom looks like her grandmother, who she never got to meet, and that's why she always comes around to play with Mom. She plays with my baby, too. Rose is helping Mom heal," Anne came in.

"Yeah. That's true," Mrs. Kate agreed.

"Well, I can't wait to see who this little angel. So, Mom, how are you doing?" Eddie asked.

"As you can see, I'm doing okay. I'm fine, and I've accepted what happened. I'm healing," Mrs. Kate answered.

"That's nice, good to hear. I'm so happy about that. We are all happy that you are with us, and we definitely can't forgive ourselves if anything should happen to you. So right now, all you have to think of is your well-being, and us too. Just know that if anything happens to you, it will affect us. So please don't overthink and take care of yourself," Eddie pleaded.

"I will. So how are your children doing?" Mrs. Kate asked.

"Well, they are okay, and they wanted to come, but I had to ask him to stay back so they could attend to some school assignments and rest. But I promise to bring them here during the holidays or probably if you can come to stay with us," Eddie explained.

"That's okay. I miss seeing them," Mrs. Kate said.

"Yeah, they miss you too. You need to see the way they were pressuring me and pleading for them to come over but I just had to ask them to stay put in the house," Eddie added.

"I think we should go outside. It's becoming a bit stuffy here. Let's talk on the balcony," Mrs. Kate said, standing up as Eddie and Anne followed behind her. The trio sat on the balcony and kept chit-chatting on family issues and other matters. Suddenly Rose appeared at the little gate that led from her parent's house. She had walked a short distance of about a quarter of a mile before getting to Mrs. Kate's place by the main gate.

Mrs. Kate tapped Eddie and pointed at her.

"Who is she?" He asked.

"That's Rose," Anne replied.

"Quite a small girl, but beautiful, lively, and cute," Eddie observed, even from that distance.

"They were still talking and laughing as they watch Rose get closer to their house but all of a sudden, a car came in from nowhere and hit Rose from behind. She fell flat on the ground as the car drove off, still at top speed.

Mrs. Kate, who saw everything that happened, shouted and fainted. Anne and Eddie were confused about who to assist first. Anne rushed outside and ran to where the accident occurred, carried Rose into her brother's car, and then ran back inside the house to help her brother move their mom into the car. Anne was about to open the front door when Eddie asked: "Where are you going to?"

"To the hospital with you, of course," Anne replied, panting.

"No, take care of your baby and inform Rose's parents of what happened," Eddie replied. He entered his car and zoomed off to the hospital. Anne ran into the house and phoned her husband, immediately telling him what happened. In less than twenty minutes, he was already home to stay with the baby as Anne rushed to inform Rose's parents of what happened and they all left for the hospital together in Stanley's car.

They got to the hospital and met Eddie leaning on the wall of the reception.

"How is Mom? How's Rose?" Anne asked, panting.

"Are they Rose's parents?" Eddie asked, pointing at the couple that came with Anne.

"Yes, we are. Where is my child, please? What happened to her and where is that reckless driver who knocked down my child?" Rose's mom asked, also still panting.

"Calm down. Rose isn't dead. Just calm down, okay?" Eddie pleaded as he held both Anne and Rose's mom by the hands.

"And where is the driver?" Rose's father asked.

"He fled the scene of the incident. He lost control as he was speeding. If he had hit Rose directly from the back, it would have been fatal, but he hit her just slightly by the side, though from the back. We all witnessed it that's why my mom fainted. You know she had grown very fond of Rose," Eddie explained as he saw the doctor coming towards them. They all rushed towards him.

"Doctor, how are they?" Eddie asked.

"Your mom is alive, but she's still in shock, and with the look of things, I don't think she will be able to make use of her legs anymore," The doctor said.

"I don't understand what you're talking about? What do you mean by that? That my mom won't be able to make use of her legs anymore? She only shouted and fainted! I mean, what has that got to do with her legs?" Anne asked.

"Your mom was shocked and had a stroke because of what happened in front of her. It affected her nervous system. I'm sorry to say this but your mother's limbs have no feelings. She will never be able to walk again," The doctor said as a matter of fact. Stanley had to take the baby from Anne as she crept to the visitor's seat by the side to sit down. She was in shock as she couldn't fathom how someone who witnessed an accident scene wouldn't be able to walk again.

"My daughter, I want to see her. I need to see my daughter," Rose's mom said, almost crying.

"I hope nothing is wrong with my daughter because if there were, I would never forgive that reckless driver, wherever he may be," Rose's father said.

"Sir, your daughter is okay. She just sustained a few bruises and some fractures which shall heal in a matter of some weeks. She's okay. There is nothing to worry about," The doctor assured.

"No problem. We need to see her, we need to see our daughter," Rose's mom said hysterically.

"Alright, you can come with me," The doctor said as all of them followed behind.

Eddie went closer to Anne, holding her by the shoulders.

"Let me just take it that the doctor is lying. It can't just be true. How could a mere shock lead to paralysis? This diagnosis looks like a fabricated story. It can't be real," Anne said as they inched nearer to the room where Rose was.

"It doesn't sound real to me either. Everything still feels like a movie on the television. You said Rose was the one who made her heal. She was the one who made her life colorful again. You said that little girl was the one who made mom happy again. Rose was able to make her move on with life. Mom had become so attached to that little girl. I think that was why Mom was shocked beyond measure at what happened. And she was coming to meet Mom. I know this is so hard to believe, but all we can do is pray for a miracle," Eddie surmised.

"Mom walked out of her room to the balcony before witnessing the accident. She only shouted and fainted. She will be okay. How can it affect her limbs?

I want to understand. No, Mom's legs aren't paralyzed. Can't you just get it?" Anne said, crying. "I don't believe it too. I'm serious. I don't believe it, but the shock might have affected Mom more than we all can imagine," Eddie admitted.

"Someone should just wake me up from this nightmare and tell me that I've been dreaming all along. Seriously, brother, how do you think our siblings will react if they should hear this? This incident is so, so confusing," Anne said.

Eddie hugged her tightly, patting her at the back so she could calm down.

"Anne," Stanley called.

Anne looked at her husband who was walking beside her with the baby in his hands.

"The shock might have affected her so much. They said that her limbs had lost some sensation, at least, it's not her whole body. She can still talk to us. Mom can still hold you and our baby. She still has her life intact. So, tell me, why the tears?" Stanley asked.

"You know Stanley sure has a point. You have to listen to him. At least Mom is alive, and it's just only her limbs, and the little girl is alive too. You know, if Rose were actually in her house, she wouldn't be in the hospital now. Rose came to see our mother. She was coming to spend time with her as usual before that fateful moment. We should be happy that they are both alive even though one will not be able to make use of her legs anymore," Eddie admitted.

"Please wipe away your tears," Stanley said, holding her with one hand while carrying the baby with the other hand.

"Yes, sister, wipe your tears. We didn't lose any life," Eddie said. Anne slowly wiped her eyes and said to her brother, "Can we go and see Mom after seeing Rose, or do we have to wait for the doctor's permission?"

After seeing Rose, they all went together to see Mrs. Kate. Mrs. Kate's eyes were wide open when they walked inside the hospital room.

"Mommy!" Anne called as she held her mother's hand tenderly.

"Is Rose okay? Is she alive?" were the first words that let Mrs. Kate's mouth.

"Of course, she is alive and well, Mom, just bruises and some fractures. Aside from that, she is okay. Her parents are with her now," Eddie said.

"She was coming to see me; she doesn't deserve this pain. Why would such a thing happen to her?" Mrs. Kate was in tears.

"Mom, please stop. She is okay, that's the most important thing," Eddie said.

"Did the doctor say anything to you?" Anne asked her mom, looking her in the eyes.

"It's about my legs, I already know. You don't need to hide it. I know that I won't be able to walk again. I know," Mrs. Kate said, smiling.

"A miracle can still happen. You never can tell. You can still work with your legs," Anne said.

"Anne, if losing my legs is the price that I'll have to pay for Rose to be alive then I will gladly give them up. She was coming to see me, remember? Had she been in her house, she would still be happy or maybe eating or even playing with her parents, but she left her place of abode just to come and make me happy. Look at the evil that befell her. I'm happy that she is alive, but I'm sad that I might never get to see her again," Mrs. Kate said.

"Don't be too sure, Mom. You will see her again. I will make sure of that," Anne said.

"Thank you," Mrs. Kate said and turned her face to the wall. She didn't want her children to see the pain she was going through.

"Mom, I'm going to leave you now. I need to take Anne back home so she can bathe her baby and feed him. I will come back later so Stanley can go back home too," Eddie said.

"That's not a problem," Mrs. Kate said without looking back. Stanley handed the baby over to Anne and she and Eddie walked out of the hospital. Eddie took off immediately. When they got to Anne's apartment, Anne exited and walked inside. Eddie called her back softly. She turned to face him.

"Please take good care of the child. Mother is going to be fine. Your husband will be back soon. I need to go home and freshen up and pick a few of my pieces of stuff. I'll be spending the night with Mom in the hospital. So, you don't have to worry," Eddie said.

"Thank you. You're a real brother. I'm proud of you," Anne said, and walked inside.

Eddie reversed his car and zoomed off as he kept thinking about what happened. Eddie saw how unpredictable life could be, that within a short time, happy moments can turn into sadness. He got home and walked into the house. His children were already asleep when he came in. Flora observed him for a second and knew that something was wrong.

"What's the problem?" She asked as he watched her husband pull off his shoes.

"It's Mom. She is going through so much pain right now," Eddie said as he finished pulling off his socks.

"How do you mean? You said Anne called and said she was doing okay. So, what happened today?" Flora asked, plainly agitated.

"It's hard to say, but Mom can't walk again," Eddie said, unbuttoning his shirt.

"This is hilarious. Please be serious. What do you mean Mom can't walk with her legs anymore?" Flora asked.

"A trip to see how my mom was doing turned out to be a trip to the hospital. A little girl who lives close to Anne's house always comes around to see Mom. She was the reason why Mom is happy again. Anne said she asked the little girl why she was so fond of her mother and said that Mom looks like her grandmother, whom she never met. She was coming to see Mom when a car hit her. We saw what happened, we witnessed the three of us: me, Mom, and Anne. The incident shocked Mom and she fainted. I rushed both mom and the girl to the hospital. Though the girl is okay with just a few bruises and fractures, the doctor said the shock affected Mom so much that her limbs became paralyzed. A few minutes ago, my mom was walking with me, and the next, she can't make use of her legs again," Eddie concluded.

Flora quietly sat down as tears trickled down her cheeks. She lowered her head to stop Eddie from knowing she was crying.

"Please don't act like Anne now. Stop crying. Mom isn't dead," Eddie pleaded.

"What are we going to do now?" Flora asked, wiping the tears off her eyes.

"I will be going back to the hospital to stay with her till tomorrow," Eddie said.

"You take care of the children while I go to the hospital instead," Flora said.

"No, don't worry. I can handle it. I don't want mom hurling insults at you in the hospital." Eddie said.

"She is free to hurl insults at me but that shouldn't stop me from taking care of her need. I should take care of her and help her out," Flora said.

"I know you have always loved my mom right from day one but don't worry, I got this, okay? Just put my dinner in my lunch bag," Eddie said and walked into the bathroom. Eddie came out and dried his body as he quickly wore his clothes, went straight to the sitting room, and took his lunch bag. He hugged his wife before leaving the house. Eddie drove off to the hospital. When he got to the hospital, he walked straight to Rose's ward to find out how she was doing.

"Good evening. Who are you?" Rose asked.

Rose's mother looked up to see who the person was.

"Good evening, ma'am." Eddie greeted.

"You can call me Stacy." Rose's mom said with a grin.

"Mom, who is he?" Rose asked again.

"It's your friend's son," Stacy replied.

"Are you Granny's child?" Rose asked.

"Yes, I am her son, and I was the one who brought you to the hospital," Eddie said.

"Why isn't she here to see me yet?" Rose asked.

"She is in this hospital with you. She will come to see you as soon as she goes home," Eddie said.

"Is she sick or what?" Rose asked, evidently alarmed.

"No, she isn't. Just that she saw what happened to you and it affected her greatly. She won't be able to walk again," Stacy said, looking away.

"You're not serious, Mom, right?" Rose said, laughing while looking at Eddie, waiting for him to refute her mom but she didn't see any sign of that.

"This isn't fair," Rose said as tears drizzled down her cheeks.

"Don't worry. Grandma will be fine. She said she is ever willing to let go of her legs for you to stay alive. Don't worry, okay, little girl. Take care," Eddie said and walked out of the room. Stacy hugged her daughter tightly as she cried profusely.

Eddie walked into his mother's ward. He asked Stanley to go home while he took over for the night. Stanley informed Eddie that Mrs. Kate managed to eat something. They bade each other goodbye as Stanley walked out of the door. Eddie focused his attention on his mom who was fast asleep. He knelt and prayed to God. The burden was much. She didn't deserve to lose her legs like that, in time of mourning her husband too.

CHAPTER FIVE

"This is tough. Since Mom doesn't like me, do you think she might allow me to take care of her?" Flora asked, looking at Eddie.

"Wait. Do you want to take care of Mom?" Eddie asked, looking at Flora, perplexed.

"Why are you surprised at me? She is my mother-in-law and I need to help her in this critical time of her life even when she was mean to me right from day one. And if I don't take care of her in our house, then who will?" Flora asked.

"Wow! You are a beautiful soul. I've always known that. I can't believe that you would even want to stay with her after all the ill-treatment meted out to you by her harsh words, the mockery? And you still want to help Mom?" Eddie said with a tinge of pride in his voice, proud that he made the right choice for his wife.

"Yes, I am going to take care of her and nurture her. She is, of course, my mother, being my mother-in-law," Flora said, smiling.

"What would I have done without you?" Eddie asked, smiling back.

"We will have to travel down to Anne's house so we can get her down to this place," Flora said.

"And that will be tomorrow. It's already late," Eddie offered.

"It's still okay with me. So, you go and have your bath while I fix your dinner. Once you finish your dinner, I will be waiting right at the dining table for you," Flora said.

"And please add sushi. I love how you prepare yours," Eddie pleaded as he made for the bathroom.

"Sure, you will get that," Flora replied, smiling as she watched her husband walk out of the bedroom into the adjoining bathroom. She made straight for the kitchen to fix dinner for her husband after having dinner that night and retired to bed. The next day, Eddie left the house very early to Anne's place to pick up his mom. When he arrived, he had a little discussion with Anne before heading to the room to meet Mrs. Kate. He opened the room door and met his mom in her wheelchair, gazing through the window. A few weeks ago, his mom was okay, and today her limbs were paralyzed.

"Good morning, Mom," Eddie greeted, forcing a smile.

Mrs. Kate turned and smiled. "How are you?" she asked.

"I am fine," Eddie said, smiling. He didn't want his mom to know that he wasn't happy seeing her in the wheelchair.

"I am here to take you home. You're going to be living with me. You know Anne's baby is still very much an infant; she can't be taking care of him and you too at the same time. Flora will take care of you," Eddie said.

"Flora can't take care of me., Mrs. Kate said, looking away.

"Do you still hate her after all these years?" Eddie asked, surprised.

"Do you want the truth?" Mrs. Kate asked.

"Of course, yes," Eddie said as he sat at the edge of the bed.

"I still have not accepted her for not being Chinese but I don't think she would even want to take care of me. I've not been nice to her. I am going to be a burden when I get there. I know I've hurt her a lot," Mrs. Kate said.

"Well, she was the one who suggested I bring you home. She willingly agreed to take care of you. I was surprised, though not so much as I know the woman I married. Your daughter-in-law is ready to take care of you. She wouldn't want anything to happen to you, even though you despised her so much. She loves you because there will be no Eddie that she could get married to without you. I don't want you to go through pain. She wants you to be happy despite your present condition. She is willing to forget all just to take care of you," Eddie said.

"I don't believe you," Mrs. Kate said.

"I know it's hard to believe, no doubt. But the truth is I can't leave you here," Eddie replied.

He stood up shortly and walked to the closet and took his time to arrange Mrs. Kate's clothes and personal property into her bags. He then took them and dropped them in his car trunk. He came back a few minutes later and wheeled her out of the room. When they got to the car, he placed her at the car seat's back before shutting the door. He opened up the car trunk and kept the wheelchair there. Anne rushed outside and opened the door to hug her mother before Eddie took her away.

"I will visit you soon," Anne assured.

"What about your baby boy?" Eddie asked.

"He is asleep. I will miss mom," Anne said as she tried to force back the tears already welling up in her eyes. Eddie drew closer to her and hugged her. Take care of yourself and your family," He whispered into her ears.

Anne wiped her tears as she watched her brother enter his vehicle and drove off.

"Anne said she would miss you, and she will visit soon," Eddie told his mom as soon as he entered the car.

"And what did you tell her?" Mrs. Kate asked.

"I told her to take care of herself and her family. Flora will continue from now on. You're my responsibility. You're my family and you're my mother," Eddie was saying when the ringing tone from his phone distracted him. As he picked it up to check who was calling him on the phone, it was Flora.

"Hey! Darling! How are you doing?" Eddie asked as soon as he picked up.

"I am okay. Are you coming back with Mom?" Flora asked.

"Of course, yes. I am coming back with Mom. We are on the road already. Can you please prepare something nice for her to eat?" Eddie asked.

"Sure. You know that's not an issue. I have already arranged the room Mom will be staying in and I've made her favorite dish," Flora replied.

"How did you get to know what her favorite dish?" Eddie was surprised.

"Remember, you once told me," Flora replied.

"It seems you're excited that Mom is coming over to our place?" Eddie asked, smiling.

"Yea. I am super excited. Ever since I got married to you, my mother-in-law hasn't visited me. I just want us to reconcile. I want to be loved by her.

I want her to see me as a daughter too, not just a mere daughter-in-law," Flora said.

"That's nice of you. We are going to be home in the next one hour thirty minutes at most," Eddie said.

"Alright, take care," said Flora.

"Flora has already prepared your favorite dish. So, get ready to eat her food once we get home. Mom, please be nice to her," Eddie pleaded.

"I will," Mrs. Kate said as Eddie looked at her twice to be sure she was the one that said so.

When they got home, Flora came outside excitedly and helped with the luggage. She took them inside the room she had prepared and kept them neatly as she watched Eddie wheel Mrs. Kate into the room.

"How are you doing, Mom?" Flora asked while standing close to her husband.

"I am fine. Thank you," Mrs. Kate replied.

Eddie brought out his phone to receive a call which just came in, after which he turned to pick up his car key.

"Where are you off to?" Flora asked.

"Got a call from the office. I need to be there in an instant. I will be back soon, and Mom, Flora, will help you out. And darling, see you soon when I'm back," Eddie said and rushed out.

Flora took a cursory look at her mother-in-law before she dashed out of the room, coming back a few minutes later with her food as she sat down close to her and started feeding her. When she finished, she gave her water to drink while she went back to the kitchen to wash the dishes. When she came back, she chit-chatted with Mrs. Kate for a while before transferring her from the wheelchair to her bed and shortly after, Mrs. Kate went into a deep sleep. Flora closed the curtains to prevent the sun from disturbing her. She took a tender loom at her once more before leaving the room.

She quietly went to the sitting room to rest. As she sat on the couch, she picked up a magazine to read. While flipping through the pages, Cynthia walked up to her and tapped her on the lap. "Good afternoon, Mommy," Cynthia said, smiling as she sat close to her mommy. Flora laid the magazine down and held her daughter tightly to her chest.

"Guess who we have here? She came in today," Flora said, smiling.

"You never told us that someone was coming to visit us. Who could that be?" Cynthia asked.

"Granny is here," Flora said, smiling.

"Yeah. I hope Grandma isn't leaving soon," Cynthia asked.

"No, she is going to stay with us for a long time," Flora told Cynthia.

"Young lady, where are you going?" Flora asked.

"I am going to Granny's room," Cynthia answered.

"Not so fast. Grandma is sleeping and you wouldn't want her to be disturbed. Don't worry, once she is awake, you can get to ask her all your questions," Flora said.

"Alright, Mommy," Cynthia answered and sat back on the chair near her mom. Flora stood up as she walked into the kitchen to prepare dinner for the family because she knows sooner or later, her husband would be back. Flora was still cooking when Cynthia informed her that the twins were awake. She left the kitchen and walked into the room, turned on the television, leaving them with their toys to play with at the same time. Flora went back into the kitchen to complete what she was doing. When she finished cooking, she switched off the cooker and went straight to the children's room to get them ready for the night.

"Cynthia, do take care of your siblings so I can attend to Grandma," Flora said when she was done with the children and walked out of the room towards Mrs. Kate's room.

When Flora got there, she discovered that she was already awake as she helped her to the bathroom to clean her up and prepare her for the night. And after that, she sat her on her wheelchair, ready for dinner. She then pushed her to the sitting room.

"Where are the children?" Mrs. Kate asked.

"They are in their room. Cynthia wanted to see you but I told her to wait while you were sleeping. Let me tell her now that you're awake," Flora offered as she left the sitting room. Once Flora informed Cynthia that Mrs. Kate was in the sitting room, she came rushing out to see her, and on seeing her, Cynthia shouted excitedly and hugged her.

"Granny, how are you doing? No one told us you were visiting. I missed you so much," Cynthia said.

"I missed you too. How are you doing? And what about the twins?" Mrs. Kate asked.

"They are with Mommy. They will soon be here. I'm doing great. I hope you're not leaving anytime soon? Mom said you're going to stay for a long time," Cynthia said.

"Yes, I am staying for a long time. So, tell me, what did I miss?" Mrs. Kate asked.

"So many things," Cynthia said, smiling, showing off her white dentition, just as Flora walked into the sitting room with Christine and Christopher. They both ran and hugged their grandma too.

"They are growing so fast? How old are they now?" Mrs. Kate asked.

"Just three years," Flora replied, smiling.

"That's lovely. How are you both doing?" Mrs. Kate asked the twins.

"Fine," they both said, almost in a whisper.

"Mom, food is ready. Should I dish out yours?" Flora asked. "Yes, sure," Mrs. Kate said as Flora walked into the kitchen to dish out the food. Soon after, she came out carrying the tray and placing it on a stool in front of Mrs. Kate, who whispered a thank you before eating.

"Cynthia, are you eating now?" Flora asked.

"No, I'm waiting for Daddy." She replied.

Flora then dished out the twin's food and quietly fed them. It was already at 7 p.m.

When Eddie returned from work, he saw how everyone talked as he walked inside the sitting room. He felt at peace knowing that his mother was already bonding well with his wife, Flora, after many years of hate.

"Daddy!" Cynthia shouted as she ran and hugged her father. She was the first to notice Eddie's presence.

"How long have you been standing here?" Flora asked.

"Long enough to know when Cynthia said, I am going to wait for Dad. You didn't want my daughter to wait for me, right?" Eddie jokingly asked.

"No, you can't be serious. Hahaha! It was already getting late and I know that you're busy with work, and it was even the third time I was asking her to eat," Flora replied, smiling.

"How are you doing, my baby girl?" Eddie asked Cynthia, holding her tenderly.

"I am doing great, Daddy, as you can see," Cynthia replied, smiling.

Eddie then went over to where his Mom was sitting and held her hands tenderly.

"How are you doing, Mommy?" Eddie asked.

"I am doing fine. Flora and the children have kept me busy," Mrs. Kate replied, smiling.

"That's lovely," Eddie said as he carried one of the twins up while the other held tightly to his Flora, his mother.

"Christopher, how are you doing?" Eddie asked.

"Fine, Daddy. Did you buy me chocolates?" He asked.

"Of course, I did, but you will have to wait for tomorrow," Eddie said.

They all prattled on about random issues for some time before Flora noticed that Christopher had fallen asleep. She then quietly took him inside and laid him on the bed, and coming back, she saw that Christine has fallen asleep in her father's hands. She took her inside their room too.

Eddie then walked inside their room to freshen up before coming out to the sitting room. Flora had already dished out his food for him and Cynthia. The duo ate as Cynthia kept asking her father numerous questions. While they were eating, Mrs. Kate informed Flora that she was feeling sleepy. Flora immediately wheeled her back to her room, helping her onto her bed and covering her with a duvet before bringing down the blinds and turning off the light. As she was about to go out of the room, she turned and said to Mrs. Kate, "Goodnight, Mother." and walked out immediately.

Eddie and Cynthia were already done with their food when she came into the sitting room, as she took the dishes to the kitchen to wash them. When she finished, she placed them where they were meant to be and walked back to the sitting room. Cynthia always slept late so Flora wasn't surprised that up till 10 p.m. she was still awake. "Cynthia, it's time to sleep. I am turning off all the appliances," Flora announced.

"I'm not feeling sleepy yet. I want to finish watching this cartoon," Cynthia protested.

"You have to sleep. Tomorrow you can continue from where you stopped." As Flora switched off the television, she took Cynthia to the children's room, laying her on the bed and covering her with the duvet. She then read bedtime stories to her and before long, she went off to sleep. Flora then kissed her three children on their foreheads before turning off the lights as she walked out of the room.

When she walked into their room, Eddie was still wide awake.

"I thought you should be asleep now," Flora said.

"I'm not feeling sleepy. I was waiting for my wife," Eddie said. "Okay. How did today go? Hope Mom didn't say anything bad to you?" Eddie asked.

"Today went well, and no, she didn't say anything bad to me, though she wasn't feeling too comfortable around me yet, which is understandable," Flora replied.

"I know. With time Mom will get used to you. Give it some time," Eddie said.

"Sure, I know. Have you called Anne yet?" Flora asked as she started to undress so she could put on her nightie.

"Yeah, sure, and she wanted to know how you're coping. We just spoke a few minutes ago before you walked into the room," Eddie said.

"That's nice. It's time to sleep. We have things to do tomorrow," Flora said as she lay on the bed beside Eddie, who cuddled her lovingly, and in no time, both were fast asleep.

Time passed and it was two years now that Mrs. Kate had been staying with Eddie. So far, they have lived peacefully. Mrs. Kate was beginning to realize the bitter truth that she had wanted to ruin a perfect relationship years ago by her unfounded bias.

On a pleasant day, she sat on the balcony couch with her wheelchair close to her. She started thinking about her life and the people she had wronged with her own words. She heard a familiar voice call out to her. As she turned to see who it was, it was Rose. She ran up to her and hugged her tightly as her life depended on it. When they disengaged from the hug, Mrs. Kate noticed some drops of tears in Rose's eyes.

"Why are you crying?" Mrs. Kate said.

"I am just happy to see you. I thought I was never going to see you again. When I came back from the hospital, I wasn't allowed to move around so I could heal, and when I got the chance to go out, Aunty Anne told me you were taken away by your son to live with him. I wanted to see you again. I wanted to see you and apologize to you but ever since then, I've not been given a chance until today. I got the freedom to come out with Anne. Grandma, can you please forgive me?" as tears trickled down her cheeks.

"Why do you want me to forgive you? You haven't done anything wrong to me. So, stop crying. There's nothing to forgive," Mrs. Kate said, drawing Rose nearer to herself.

"I am the cause of everything. I was the one who made you be in this condition. I am sorry. If I had stayed in my house, this wouldn't have happened. Can you please forgive me?" Rose pleaded even more.

Mrs. Kate was bewildered by Rose's selflessness. "You're not the cause of my predicament. You were not the one that made me faint when I witnessed the accident. You were coming to see me, to make me feel happy, remember? So, my dear, stop blaming yourself. What happened could be attributed to fate, nothing more. Please, you don't have to be sad over anything," Mrs. Kate pleaded.

"Are you sure about that?" Rose asked.

"I am more than sure, my dear." Mrs. Kate said and hugged her.

"Wow! I am just speechless. She had a desire to see you ever since you returned from the hospital but her parents wouldn't let her go far, and today is her birthday. Rose made a wish to see you and that's why she is here with me," Anne explained.

"Thank you so much, Aunty Anne. You made it possible," Rose said, smiling.

"You're welcome, my dear," Anne said, smiling back. At that instant, Flora came out of the house to see who the people were speaking. She saw Anne and hugged her tightly.

"How are you doing? You didn't come with Dennis?" Flora asked.

"Dennis went out with his dad so I had to come alone. His dad insisted on staying with him today," Anne explained.

"That's nice. Talk of son-father bonding," Flora said.

"Aunty Anne!" Cynthia shouted as she hugged Anne tightly. The twins came out and hugged her too.

"What are you feeding them? They are growing so fast," Anne observed.

"Just food, my dear," Flora said, smiling.

"Is she your daughter?" Cynthia asked as she pointed at Rose.

"She is Granny's friend," Anne answered.

"Really?" Cynthia said. And on turning to Rose, she asked,

"What is your name?"

"I am Rose, and you?"

"Cynthia."

"You're Grandma's friend?" Cynthia asked.

"Yes," Rose answered.

"Hmmm." Cynthia looked surprised, obviously wondering how a small girl could be her grandma's friend.

"Are you surprised?" Anne chimed in.

"Yes, sure," Cynthia admitted.

"That's one of those things in life. Friendship defies age difference," Flora added as she pushed the wheelchair towards Mrs. Kate, helping her sit on it before moving her inside the sitting room. She helped her sit on the couch as they all kept prattling on random issues, during which Rose didn't fail to remind Mrs. Kate how she missed her and all of their fun times together. Eventually, Flora served all of the food in the sitting room as they all ate like one big family.

"This is delicious," Rose observed, smiling.

"My mom is one of the best cooks ever, an excellent cook," Cynthia commented very proudly.

"Remind me how old are you again?" Flora asked Rose.

"I am ten," Rose replied as she gulped down the glass of water close to her.

"She talks and reasons like an adult, right?" Anne asked Flora, looking at her directly.

"Sure. That's why I asked her age," Flora said.

They were still in the spirit of celebration when Eddie came back home, and again, they didn't notice his presence because they were busy talking and laughing.

"Am I missing anything here?" Eddie said, drawing attention to himself.

"Come and sit down, Daddy. Let me tell you what you missed so far," Cynthia said, smiling.

"You came back home early," Flora observed.

"Yea, because I finished the day's work on time," Eddie answered as he went and sat close to his daughter, Cynthia.

"My princess, what's happening? Talk to Daddy," Eddie said. "Granny's friend Rose came by with Aunty Anne. We were only talking and laughing like family, and we even had lunch here. You missed so much, Daddy," Cynthia replied.

"Your daughter sure knows how to give details of things that happened, just like her father," Anne said, laughing.

"Oh, yes. That's why she is Daddy's princess," Eddie replied, smiling.

"How are you, Mom?" Eddie asked, directing his attention to Mrs. Kate.

"As you can see, I am doing great," Mrs. Kate replied, smiling.

"Great. Anne, what of your baby? Isn't he here with you?" Eddie asked.

"Dennis is over three years now. His dad wanted to spend time with him today so they both went out to be back in the evening. By then, I should be already home," Anne replied.

"That's cool. Rose, how are you doing?" Eddie asked.

"Do you still remember me?" Rose asked.

"Of course, I do remember you, though it's been two years now. Countless times I visited Anne to see you and know how you're doing but I couldn't get the chance to do so," Eddie explained.

"It's because Mom and Dad wouldn't let me go out. However, today happens to my birthday and my parents swore to grant me anything I want. I told them I wish to spend the day with Grandma and they agreed. So, they took me to Aunty Anne, and here we are today. I missed Grandma so much," Rose said, smiling.

"Is today your birthday?" Cynthia asked.

"Yes, Cynthia. Today is my birthday," Rose answered.

"Daddy, we should get her chocolates and muffins for her birthday when she is leaving," Cynthia suggested.

"That's a nice suggestion. We all will go out together but it's late now. I can give money to Anne to get it for her," Eddie said.

"That is still okay," Cynthia replied.

"Alright. I am heading to my room to bathe and change into something light. I'll be out in a few minutes," Eddie said, standing up as he went inside his room. Flora had to leave to the kitchen to prepare and dish out her husband's food. She warmed the food and kept it on the dining table with a glass of water. When Eddie came out, he watched his family chatting amidst laughter. This was what he wanted though it took time before it started happening.

Eddie was happy his mom was beginning to like Flora and seeing her as a daughter. He had thought bringing his mom to the house would brew further animosity between her and his wife but it was the opposite. Instead, the mother-daughter bonding was being fostered between them. He knew Flora was happy with the development because she had always wanted the love of her mother-in-law. When he finished his food, he joined his family in the sitting room. While there, he carried one of the twins while he was chipping into their discussion once in a while. It clocked 5 p.m. when Anne informed them that they would soon be leaving to get home on time. Eddie dipped his hand into his pocket and gave her some money to buy gifts for Rose. After the hugs and goodbyes, Anne and Rose left the house.

"I love your friend, Granny," Cynthia said.

"She is a nice girl," Mrs. Kate added.

"But why would Rose's parents ask her not to come and visit you?" Cynthia asked.

"Stop asking questions," Flora cautioned.

"Never mind, my dear. Little children are always inquisitive. I will answer her," Mrs. Kate said.

"So, tell me, Granny," Cynthia said, chuckling.

"She had an accident while she was coming to see me when I was still living with Anne. She was bedridden for months so her joints and bones could heal. The bruises healed quickly, but the bones took time. Her parents didn't ban her from seeing me, they just wanted their daughter to heal properly. Any parents out there in their shoes will do the same to their daughter," Mrs. Kate answered.

"Did you also have an accident?" Cynthia asked.

"Cynthia!" Flora shouted.

"Allow her, Flora," Mrs. Kate said.

"So, tell me, Granny," Cynthia said.

"Well, when I witnessed what happened to Rose, I was in shock and fainted because I was so attached to her. I was taken to the hospital by your dad and that was when the doctor told him that the shock made me have a stroke. It affected my limbs, and I could never be able to walk again," Mrs. Kate replied.

"Don't worry, Granny. You will walk again," Cynthia said.

"Thank you, dear," Mrs. Kate said, smiling.

Later that night, they all went to bed with Flora making sure that Mrs. Kate was well tucked away in her bed, ready to sleep, before retiring to their room and meeting her husband still awake.

"You're still awake?" Flora asked as she walked into the room.

"Yes, I am," Eddie replied.

"I am just happy that you're bonding well with mother and she has now come to realize you're the perfect daughter-in-law," Eddie said.

"Yes, though it took her years to realize, I am happy that at least we can sit and talk and laugh," Flora said.

"Thank you for everything you're doing. Not everyone would do this. You're just the exact definition of an angel," Eddie said, smiling.

"Thanks, my dear husband, my armored knight," Flora replied as she placed her hand on her husband's head, and in a few minutes after reminiscing on a sundry issue, they were both off to sleep.

Time sure flies fast. It was already eight years now that Mrs. Kate had been living with his son and daughter-in-law. On this morning, Flora had walked into Mrs. Kate's room to help her when she discovered her temperature was very high.

"Mom, you're sick. Let me get some medicine for you," Flora said.

"Don't worry, Flora," Mrs. Kate said.

"Why? But you're sick. Why shouldn't I worry?" Flora asked.

"Flora, the first day you came into this house when my son introduced you to me as his fiancée, I was happy, but that happiness became eroded when I heard you weren't Chinese. I never wanted any of my children to marry someone from a different country; that was my desire. On several occasions, I fought tooth and nail to make sure Eddie ditched you for someone else but the love was stronger. His love for you prevailed. I mistreated you and yet after all the ill-treatment meted to you by me and the harsh words said to you, you didn't stop loving me. You loved me the way you loved your mother, volunteering to take care of me although you had three children to cater to. You took all the responsibilities and never once did you complain. You made me realize that true love can never be broken. You made me realize that you were the angel I wanted to lose years ago because of some stupid reason. For eight years now, you single-handedly took care of me without complaining, with smiles. Thank you, Flora, and I hope you can find a place in your heart to forgive me," Mrs. Kate said, smiling.

"You didn't do anything to me and I never for one day bore any grudges towards you. So, there is no need to apologize. You might not be my biological mother, but you're my husband's mother. You brought him into this world, and I am forever grateful for that," Flora said with a wide grin.

"I have seen you and Ed all of these years keeping to yourselves, for better or worse, in sickness and in health, and I know until death do you part, you two will remain attached to each other. You are indeed his Hawaiian soul mate," Mrs. Kate whispered as Flora smiled.

Mrs. Kate smiled back and closed her eyes, and when Flora touched her, she wasn't breathing. She rushed out to call Eddie, who came in and one look at his mom told him she had passed. Flora threw herself on the floor and let the tears freely flow down her cheeks. She had wanted more time with Mrs. Kate, to make up for the years she wasn't on good terms with her. When Flora gathered herself up, she got up, kissed Mrs. Kate on the forehead, bidding her eternal farewell to the great beyond.

ABOUT THE AUTHOR

Dennis W.C. Wong, was born in Honolulu, Oahu, territory of Hawaii in 1951 at Kapiolani Hospital. His Family moved to San Francisco in 1958.

Mr. Wong had a BS degree in Business Management – Personnel and Industrial Relationship at California State University, Hayward.

Currently, Mr. Wong works at Kaiser Permanente in Oakland, CA as a Nurse Assistant in the Operating Room Department and became a Licensed Vocational Nurse doing some healthcare. Also, as a Sterile Processing Technician, Mr. Wong volunteers with Surgical missions to Guatemala and Ecuador.

Mr. Wong's previous two books are "The Apricot Outlook of Kathering Koon Hung Wong" and "The App I Cot Journey to Plumville – Empowering Kids to Overcome Adversity". His passion continues in "The Power of Passion".

CPSIA information can be obtained
at www.ICGtesting.com
Printed in the USA
FSHW011949110521
81383FS